T0072845

BOUND
FOR
TROUBLE

BOUND
FOR TROUBLE

BDSM EROTICA FOR WOMEN

EDITED BY
ALISON TYLER

CLEIS
PRESS

Copyright © 2014 by Pretty Things Press.

All rights reserved. Except for brief passages quoted in newspaper, magazine, radio, television, or online reviews, no part of this book may be reproduced in any form or by any means, electronic or mechanical, including photocopying or recording, or by information storage or retrieval system, without permission in writing from the publisher.

Published in the United States by Cleis Press, Inc., 2246 Sixth Street, Berkeley, California 94710.

Printed in the United States.
Cover design: Scott Idleman/Blink
Cover photograph: © Steve Kraitt/cultura/Corbis
Text design: Frank Wiedemann

First Edition.
10 9 8 7 6 5 4 3 2 1

Trade paper ISBN: 978-1-62778-027-8
E-book ISBN: 978-1-62778-044-5

All June I bound the rose in sheaves,
Now, rose by rose, I strip the leaves.

—Robert Browning

Contents

INTRODUCTION

*B*ondage. I still get a shiver down my spine when I say that word. I love the way the hard *B* sounds. I love the images that bloom in my mind when I consider what the term encompasses.

Believe it or not, this is my tenth bondage-themed collection for Cleis Press. (Where did the time go?) From *Best Bondage Erotica* to *Slave to Love* to *Hurts So Good*, I have been a busy little editor, collecting the very best BDSM stories for your pleasure.

With *Bound for Trouble* I've uncovered new jewels, glimmering examples of the ultimate in erotic writing. Every writer in this book focuses on a different facet of the bondage theme. Some characters use tools, some words, one uses paper chains. There are male subs and femme-dommes and the reverse. But what these writers have in common is the same type of fascination that I have with the theme. I am addicted. Obsessed. Plain and simple, I'm bound for trouble.

To Sophia Valenti, bondage means:

> *Perfectly still. That's how I wanted him. Unable to move, unable to speak. Unable to schedule yet another meeting or conference call. I wanted him to stop moving and be fully present in the moment, instead of rushing through it because he was already planning the next one.*

To Tamsin Flowers, bondage means:

> *I'm half kneeling on the bed, with my face in the pillows and my arse in the air. With a rip my panties are gone. I feel his hands slowly caress my naked buttocks and a shiver of anticipation runs through me.*

To Teresa Noelle Roberts, bondage means:

> *A length of soft rope, cooler than the warm June air, passed over the bare skin of my belly. I sighed and leaned back against him. He was shirtless but still had jeans on, and the contrasting textures of denim and furred skin, along with the texture of the rope, pushed away the day's petty concerns. "We're trying something new tonight," he purred in my ear.*

To Kiki DeLovely, bondage means:

> *She regards me with such intensity I feel desperately vulnerable and still somehow safe enough to let her in. Though she needs no invitation. Lux fully knows this is hers for the taking. So she takes it and I accept*

*my role as a willing sacrifice, laying my body down
before her. I allow her to forge away at her own pace;
accept whatever is left when she is done. Her eyes
taste every last curve.*

To Rachel Kramer Bussel, bondage means:

*I tried to prepare myself for the rush of blood about
to flood my tender flattened buds, but you can never
truly be ready. That's part of the thrill of kink for
me—the unexpected, the way even the most familiar
activity can catch you off guard, make you feel like a
virgin all over again as the pain crashes down.*

To Andrea Dale, bondage means:

*To be tied down—or strapped or chained or what-
ever—was the crucial act. To be made to believe I
was helpless. (I wouldn't be, with the safeword, but
still.) Helpless to whatever she wanted to do to me,
pain or pleasure. Helpless to whatever she wanted
me to do: come or not come, react or wait in excruciating anticipation.*

Each writer approaches this subject in a bold, unique way—
but all of the stories are tied together with one chrome-colored
theme: bondage.

Flip the pages. Choose a story. Whether you're an aficionado
like myself, or a neophyte to this dark, velvet world, get ready
to be *Bound for Trouble*.

XXX,
Alison

TEA OR COFFEE?

Tamsin Flowers

So, hell, now I find myself hog-tied, wrists bound to ankles with silky red rope, in the swanky riverside apartment of some guy that, until just over an hour ago, I'd never laid eyes on. All I've got on is a pair of black lace panties and a pair of Rupert Sanderson stilettos, having left my dignity somewhere over by the door. I've never been tied up before, I've never been spanked before and I've certainly no idea what's going to happen next. And I have to say, I think I'm enjoying myself. But how the fuck did I get myself into this in the first place?

I think it was something I said.

Tonight was an evening that came with expectations built in. An expectation of meeting someone, the anticipation of excitement or of disappointment, a feeling that one thing might lead to another. Speed dating. It wasn't my first time but it was definitely the first time that the one thing had actually led to another. Previous outings on the speed-dating merry-go-round had been underwhelming but, eternal optimist that I am, I couldn't see any harm in giving it another go and—hey presto—it seems to have delivered.

This is how it went down. The first two guys that sat in the hot seat opposite me were dull. One was tongue-tied, while the other couldn't stop talking. About himself. The third man was nice but ancient. The fourth, good looking but weird. But the fifth was interesting. Tall, I noticed as he approached my table. Confident, authoritative, he had the air of someone used to being in control. He sat down and gave me an appraising look; there was no trying to hide the fact that he was looking me over, checking me out. I might not have liked a look like that in a different situation but I wasn't gonna kid myself—this is what we were both here for, after all.

I looked him up and down, too, and he was some physical specimen. Strong jaw, broad shoulders, beautiful hands and a luxuriant head of burnished copper hair. His dark eyes held mine until I felt compelled to look away.

"What's your name?"

"Vayle. Yours?"

"Lucas."

Our eyes met once again. There was a certain intensity to his stare that made me want to find out more about him. Made me want to touch him or see him without his clothes.

"What do you do?" I said.

"Tea or coffee?"

"I'm sorry?"

"Do you drink tea or coffee?" His voice held a note of impatience.

"Coffee."

"Whisky or gin?"

"Gin."

"Chanel or Prada?"

"Prada."

"Negligee or naked?"

"Naked."

There was no pause between questions, no time for me to consider the answers I was giving. It was like a game of word association and I was happy to play along.

"Oral or anal?"

I faltered for a second and then said "Both."

"Top or bottom?"

"Bottom."

Lucas suddenly stood up.

"Come on, let's get out of here," he said, holding out a hand to me.

I glanced around the room. The other participants were busy talking as fast as they could to get in all they needed to say before their four minutes ran out. The man at the table next to mine, my next prospect in other words, was ugly beyond ugly. Lucas was good looking and unpredictable.

"I'm with you," I said, pulling my coat off the back of my chair and grabbing my bag.

So that's how it all started. He took me to a bar and ordered me a gin and tonic.

"Drink it," he said, already halfway through his.

He ordered us each another. There was no doubt who was in control. Lucas set the agenda, and I was content to sit back and enjoy the ride.

"I'd like you to come back to my apartment," he said. "Would you consider it?"

I knew what that meant. He wanted to have sex with me. And after two gins and a month-long sex drought, I wanted to have sex with him. He seemed like someone who would know what he was doing.

Lucas did know what he was doing and now I'm lying on my back on his bed, tied up and virtually naked. He walks across the room toward me, still fully dressed in a crisp white shirt and sharply tailored gray trousers. He's taken off his shoes and socks and his belt is undone, flapping around the waistband of his pants. He has thoroughly kissed me and I have allowed him to undress me and tie me up. I feel sexually charged, wet and ready for his pleasure and mine.

He stands over me, looking down, and I can read naked lust in his eyes.

"Safeword?" he says.

More word association?

"Firebreak."

Then he flips me over, so now I'm half kneeling on the bed, with my face in the pillows and my arse in the air. With a rip my panties are gone. I feel his hands slowly caress my naked buttocks and a shiver of anticipation runs through me.

"God, you have a beautiful arse," he says.

Warm juices are pooling high in my cunt and I know that if I shift my position, they'll flood down my leg. I hold as still as I can, relishing the thought of how that's going to feel. But then Lucas trails a finger down my arsecrack and round to the soft folds of flesh between my legs. He discovers the reservoir of my desire and I hear his breath hitching in his throat.

"You're so ready to play, aren't you?"

"Yes," I say. "So ready."

And he uses his hand to spread my wetness forward to my clit, which hardens at his brief touch, and back between my buttocks, making me arch my back to push them higher in the air.

"There's only one thing I can do to a beautiful arse like yours," he whispers, his face close to my ear as one hand runs down my back in a long stroke.

"It's all yours," I say. "Do what you need to."

Lucas steps away from me and bends to open a drawer in the bedside cabinet. I hear him rifling through stuff and wonder what he's doing; looking for a condom, I hope, a little belatedly given my situation. But when he straightens up, it's not a condom that he has in his hand. It's a red leather paddle and he's using his other hand to test its flexibility. He slaps it against his palm a couple of times; the slapping noise has some weight behind it and deep inside me muscles clench. Goose bumps rise and I would be lying if I said I'm not scared. But at the same time I'm excited, more excited and more turned on than I can ever remember being.

I shut my eyes and bite my lip, waiting for the first slap. A soft caress of my left buttock takes me by surprise and relaxes me a split second before the paddle makes contact with my right. I gasp as the sting radiates through my flesh, leaving a burn on the surface and a spasm deep within. A cool hand assuages the burning sensation, but then my left buttock falls victim to the paddle's bite. I shriek at the shock of it as it burns a path through me, waking up feelings and desires, making me shiver as I realize I want to feel it again.

And it comes again, on the other side once more, adding another layer of pain, building on the last one, and then again, like a series of seismic waves, shaking me to the core. I'm breathing fast as a firestorm grows between my legs; each soft caress Lucas administers between the blows becomes torture in its own right as I push back against his hand, willing it to stay there, to press harder, to slide down between my cheeks, to press his way into me, into my arse, into my cunt, to fill me up as my muscles clench around him, as I reach that perfect moment...but he doesn't do it. He withdraws his hand and replaces it with the sting and bite of the paddle, making me cry out again or making me bite my lip.

"This is what you wanted, isn't it?" he whispers in my ear at one point.

"Yes," I hiss.

And I realize that he's right. I might not have known it before; it was beyond the realm of my experience. But this is what I've needed all along. This is what's been missing so far. The thoughts blur as the pain builds and the longing for fulfillment sweeps over me again and again.

Then I hear the paddle drop to the floor. In the silence that follows, I can hear Lucas breathing heavily, either with the exertion or excitement. Both I think. He pulls something from the drawer. A condom this time; I hear the rip of the package. Seconds later, the soft firm nudge of his cock. He guides it up and down between my buttocks and then lets it slide down and lie along the folds of my labia. I push myself against it, moaning softly with my need to feel it plunging deep inside.

"Where would you like it, babe?" he says.

He teases me with a finger, first sliding it slickly into my cunt and then, once it's wet and slippery, easing it into my butt, making me gasp loudly. It feels so good both times I can't decide.

"Wherever you like," I say.

"Good answer," he says. "But first I'm going to untie you."

Seconds later my wrists are free and Lucas places my hands gently on the top of the headboard.

"Hold tight," he instructs.

I do as I'm bid, stretching my back up; I'm still kneeling on the bed, holding the headboard, awaiting his pleasure. He's kneeling on the bed behind me. He uses a hand to spread my legs wide and I feel his fingers parting my labia. Then, ever so slowly, he pushes the tip of his cock upward into my cunt. He's large, one of the largest I've ever had, and it's a good, tight fit.

With his hands on my shoulders, he rams it home, and then his hands slide round my sides to cup my breasts. He pulls me back against him and starts rolling his hips to draw himself in and out. Now my body's arching against his as his big cock grazes its way up and down against the sweet spot inside.

An orgasm starts to bubble softly as he sweeps in and out. Then suddenly he changes the game. Lucas pushes me forward and his hands pull my buttocks wide apart. From somewhere he grabs lube and I feel a shock of cold down the length of my crack; his fingers getting me ready. Without a change in the rhythm, he pushes his cock into my yielding arse. My orgasm explodes on the first stroke, making my muscles clench hard around him. With a cry as loud as my own, he comes, his cock surging and throbbing within me. I can feel its heat and I can feel the pulse of his climax, the sensations stoking my own. My body spasms again and then the heat starts to dissipate.

I feel limp and wrung out, and there's a final bite of pain as he pulls out his cock. We slump together on the bed, our bodies slick with sweat, awash with the smell of sex. I wait for the pulses to subside and slowly my breathing returns to normal. Lucas, still panting, peels off the rubber and drops it over the side of the bed. Then he flips me onto my back and straddles me. His face is serious as he looks down on me.

"You'd never been spanked before, had you?"

I shake my head, still not trusting myself to talk.

"You'd never been tied up?"

"No."

"You've had no experience of domination and submission?"

"No."

"Did you know you could have stopped me with your safe-word?"

I swallow.

"I didn't want you to stop. I wanted it to go on."

His eyes soften.

"When I asked you, 'Top or bottom?' what did you think I meant?"

"Top or bottom bunk."

I feel stupid.

He climbs off me and off the bed, walking over to the window. The lights of the city are spread out before him.

"Lucas?" I whisper. "Don't send me away."

He turns around and his eyes still have the soft expression.

"You'll need to be trained. I want a lover who's willing to wear my collar. Could you do that?"

I don't know what he means, but I want to find out.

"Yes, Lucas. Please train me."

So that's how it went down on that evening of expectations. It was all due to something I said. I wonder what would have happened if I'd said "top"?

SIMPLE PLEASURES

Sophia Valenti

Perfectly still. That's how I wanted him. Unable to move, unable to speak. Unable to schedule yet another meeting or conference call. I wanted him to stop moving and be fully present in the moment, instead of rushing through it because he was already planning the next one.

I understood where he was coming from, I really did. Marco was a busy man. His life was a maelstrom of appointments. Between meetings, travel, and business engagements masquerading as social events, it was a wonder we found any time to date. Though I'll admit that sometimes he managed to fit me in by double booking. Trust me, I'd gone to my fair share of corporate shindigs, during which I'd smile and make polite conversation that was only interrupted when impossibly slender wannabe actors would wander by with trays of tiny food. The servers would flash their professionally whitened smiles, but when I looked into their eyes, I could tell they'd rather be somewhere else. It was similar to the look of longing I'd see in Marco's eyes at the end of a tiring day, when he'd let his guard down. I knew he loved his work, but he was wrapped up in a tangle of obligations. Having taken control of his family's business, he was determined to make it even more successful than it had already been. Pride and ambition fueled him, but he didn't know how to switch off those feelings in order to recharge.

The world may have seen a bold, successful executive, but I saw a man who desperately needed someone else to take the reins—if only for a little while.

I'd seen glimmers of that desire the times I'd wrested control from him in the bedroom. The first time I flipped us over and rode his cock, I saw his eyes light with fire. The next time, I took things a step further, holding his wrists over his head as I ground my body against him and took my pleasure. I watched his face soften as he surrendered to my will and lost himself in pure, unadulterated lust.

I felt like his true nature had been revealed to me for the very first time, and it tripped something inside me. I wanted to see that look again. I wanted him exposed and vulnerable, abandoning everything he thought he needed to be.

While he may have lavished me with expensive presents, that moment of clarity and release would be my gift to him.

To date, every one of our sexual encounters had taken place at his luxurious penthouse suite, but for my plan to be successful, I needed to take him out of that space. It would only remind him of every responsibility he needed to forget.

Every time we spoke during the week I was mulling my seduction, I was more tight-lipped than usual. Mainly because I was having a hard time making polite conversation. My mind was busy conjuring up different scenarios that would end with Marco in my thrall. I could see him—leather cuffs wrapped around his wrists, hands chained overhead. That lone image haunted me, fueling my lust at inopportune times, like when Marco called to ask me what I wanted to do that night.

It was clear that he'd sensed something was on my mind, and he was eager to head off what he perceived as an impending problem. That's my Marco—a man of action. His response to my aloof behavior was to clear his entire evening. He made a point of letting me know that night would be solely about the two of us. I let his announcement hang in the air. Before responding, I wanted to savor the fact that he'd rearranged his schedule for me—and let his discomfort last a few seconds longer. He seemed so eager to please me, and I got an indecent thrill from the notion.

After a long pause, I told him I'd love to spend the night with him. Marco then tossed off the names of a half-dozen ultraexclusive restaurants, but I shot down each suggestion. He seemed confused.

"I was thinking something more cozy. Like, say, Chinese takeout on my living room floor."

He laughed softly. "That sounds perfect."

I knew it would be.

This would be the first time Marco got a good look at my apartment. It was a midsized studio that was more than enough room for me, even though it was more like a walk-in closet to most people in his social circles. But it did have certain amenities that his luxury building lacked—like eyebolts in the headboard.

I didn't point those out to Marco, though. He'd be aware of them soon enough. I wanted him to relax, so he'd be open to what I was about to offer him—a temporary escape from all that weighed on him. It seemed he was already on his way. He looked casual and comfortable that night, having traded his usual uniform of a custom-made suit for a white button-down and faded jeans. His normally perfect hair was a little less so, and the first few buttons of his shirt were open, revealing a patch of caramel-colored skin dusted with dark hair.

We had a relaxing dinner, sitting cross-legged and barefoot on my living room rug. Marco leaned back against the couch, wineglass in hand, gazing at me without speaking.

"What's up? You have that look in your eye."

"Thanks," he said softly.

"For what?"

"For this. For something so...simple."

"I think simple pleasures are the most satisfying."

I brought my hand to his cheek, stroking it and feeling the barest hint of stubble scratch my fingertips. He turned his face, kissing my palm, and his warm, soft lips made my flesh tingle at their touch.

"The night's not over, though," I added.

"God, I hope not." Marco's dark brown eyes glowed with passion.

"Then come," I told him, rising to my feet and offering him my hand. He stood and let me lead him across the room to my bed.

His hands immediately went to me, eager to strip off my dress.

"No, baby—my place, my rules. Hands at your sides."

Marco seemed startled by my request, but he obeyed, his lips curling into a smile.

"Yes, Ma'am," he replied teasingly.

"Mmm, I like the sound of that."

I took my time unbuttoning his shirt and slipping it off his shoulders, sliding my hands down his muscular arms to caress his toned, tanned flesh. My hands lingered at his waistband as I leaned in for a kiss. He lifted his arms as if to embrace me, then remembered my command and snapped them back to his sides.

"Good boy," I murmured against his lips.

A growl came from deep in his throat, and he kissed me roughly. His tongue was aggressive, diving between my lips. I could tell that he was struggling to keep his hands where they were, but the fact that he did made me ache for him. I felt the pulse of arousal beating deep inside me, escalating with every second he complied. I grabbed the back of his head, tangling my fingers in his thick, wavy hair to hold him in place. With my lips pressed to his, I felt the change within him. His aggression melted, transforming into a burgeoning tension brimming with unfulfilled need. His desire for me was still just as strong, but he held himself in check, even as his yearning increased a hundredfold.

Breathless, I pulled away, and we stared at each other for a heartbeat.

"So, do you have any other rules I need to know about?"

"Well, the most important one is that I'm in charge."

Rising up on my toes, I kissed his cheek and leaned closer to whisper in his ear. "And that means you're my plaything for the night." Marco drew in a deep breath, seeming to hold it as he waited for me to continue. "That means I'm going to strip you down and cuff you to my bed. Use you for my pleasure. And if I'm satisfied, maybe—just maybe—I'll let you come."

Marco exhaled with a groan.

I brought my hand to the front of his jeans, feeling his erection as hard as ever beneath the well-worn denim. I cupped his bulge and gave it a gentle squeeze.

"It seems my plan agrees with you."

"Yes, yes, it does," he murmured.

"Yes...?"

"Yes...Ma'am."

"There you go," I said softly.

Reaching under my dress, I slid off my panties. They were already damp, merely from me telling him what I wanted to do to him. I balled up the satin and brought it to his face. "Open," I commanded, tucking the moist scrap of fabric between his parted lips. Marco's eyes fluttered closed for a moment, and I smiled. That's what I wanted. I wanted his world to stop; I wanted him to focus on what he was feeling both physically and emotionally. I knew this was new territory for him; he was used to being the man who made all the decisions. But there were no decisions to make, other than the one to submit. Having already made that commitment, he was completely free.

Marco clenched and unclenched his fists as I unfastened his jeans and slid them down. His hard cock sprang free, but I didn't touch it—no matter how tempting it was. There would be time for that later. As he stood before me, naked and vulnerable, I let my eyes roam over his body. His formidable muscles were tense with lust and anticipation. He could have stopped me at any time, but it thrilled me that he chose not to.

With a gentle hand on his chest, I backed him toward my bed. He kicked away his clothing and let me direct him, settling himself where I wanted him in the center of the mattress. He lay on his back against the ebony comforter, and I straddled his hips. I was keenly aware of his erection—hot and hard—just inches beneath my naked slit. I was sure he could feel the heat emanating from my slick, wet sex. I pulled my dress over my head and tossed it aside, finally as naked as he was. My pale pink panties were still wedged between his lips, and I leaned forward, flicking my tongue against them. Marco uttered a muffled groan that was laced with frustration.

Reaching under the pillow, I pulled out a set of leather cuffs. They were soft and supple but would hold him fast.

"Hands," I commanded, and Marco didn't delay, offering me his wrists. The sound of metal against metal as I buckled the cuffs into place made my cunt clench with anticipation. After kissing each of his hands in tender acknowledgment of him putting his trust in me, I raised his arms overhead, attaching each cuff's clip to an eyebolt embedded in my wooden headboard. Marco gave a small tug, but his hands went nowhere. He exhaled and briefly closed his eyes, his resignation fueled by relief and absolute surrender. He seemed more at peace than I'd ever known him to be.

I lowered my body, pressing his stiff cock against his stomach as I trapped it between us. Rather than taking him inside me, I rocked my hips forward and back, riding the length of his shaft. With my hands pressed firmly to his chest, I writhed above him, my dance fueled solely by my desire. Tilting my body just so, I was able to get the pressure and friction against my clit that I craved.

As I worked my body in a perfect rhythm, I kept my eyes locked on Marco's. The lust and desperation that were reflected back at me only served to excite me further. His face and chest were flushed, but he kept his body rigid and still. The beautiful boy—he was playing by my rules. He was letting me use his handsome body to work myself closer and closer to climax. I felt the pleasure rising, flooding my body until it burst in a bright explosion of ecstasy.

I was loud when I came, crying out and squeezing my thighs against his body. When the last wave washed over me, I collapsed against Marco, crushing my breasts against his heaving chest.

After yanking the panties from his lips, I kissed him deeply. I heard the clicking of metal overhead as he tugged at his cuffs, and I smiled against his mouth. Reaching back, I took hold of his cock, so slick and hot. With deliberate slowness, I lowered myself onto his shaft, taking him in deep. My cunt clenched around him, and Marco's cuffs rattled once more. I could see the conflicted feelings flashing across his face. I knew he wanted to ram up into me, to take what he so desperately desired. But he'd promised to let me be in control—and deep down he liked that. So he obeyed. He lay as still as possible and surrendered to the pleasure that filled him as I rose and fell, riding him until he groaned with abandon and came inside me. All of that sublime tension in his body disappeared as he let himself go and focused on nothing but bliss.

Afterward, in between heavy breaths, Marco dared to speak.

"You're right."

"About what?" I asked, trailing my fingers down his chest.

"Simple pleasures *are* the most satisfying."

PAPER CHAINS

Annabeth Leong

Malinda knew Lorrie well enough to read her mood by the way she chewed her cereal. She sat in the chair next to her wife and poured herself a bowl to match. "Spill," Malinda said.

Lorrie put down her spoon and blinked. With her angelic face and wavy blonde hair, the innocent act would have worked if Malinda hadn't seen it a hundred times before.

Malinda narrowed her eyes. "Come on. You're obliterating those poor cornflakes. What's going on?" Then she looked away to give Lorrie a little space.

Malinda toyed with the salt and pepper shakers they'd gotten from their wedding registry a year ago and stroked the petals of the pink anniversary roses she'd given Lorrie earlier that morning. She had a complicated, extravagant evening planned. In her gut, she feared she would overwhelm Lorrie, who so frequently seemed fragile. Malinda still could not bear to cancel any of it. She could not master her need to make Lorrie happy, to give her anything and everything necessary.

Lorrie gave the little shrug that meant something was definitely wrong. Malinda took a bite of her own cereal and chewed as slowly as she could to give her wife plenty of time. Lorrie responded much better to patience than to repeated requests.

The third bite in, she finally talked. "I don't want to go to that restaurant tonight."

"I'll cancel the reservation," Malinda said immediately. "We can go wherever you like." She smiled and offered her best compromise. "I'll even take you for sushi if you want."

Lorrie shook her head, her blue eyes hidden behind feathery wisps of her hair. "It's not just that restaurant, though I appreciate the offer of sushi." She sighed. "I don't really want to go to a restaurant. I want to do something really special for our anniversary."

"I'm going to make sure it's special, I promise."

Lorrie pushed the cereal bowls out of the way, then touched the back of Malinda's hand. "That's just it, Malinda. I want to do something special. For you. For once."

Malinda forced herself to meet her wife's gaze. She'd started to understand what this was about. "Lorrie, I like the way things are. I don't need anything from you."

"I know. Believe me." Tears trembled at the corners of Lorrie's eyes. She looked so tired and defeated that Malinda's heart broke a little.

"Hey," Malinda said. She kissed Lorrie's cheek quickly, before she could allow her nerves to create distance between them. This was not how she'd wanted their anniversary to go, but if one year of marriage had taught her anything, it was that tears and fights seemed to come most reliably at the times they felt obligated to "be happy."

Malinda searched herself, trying to figure out why she

resisted so strenuously when Lorrie wanted to do something for her. "What did you have in mind?"

"I want to tie you up and make you come."

Malinda's heart dropped into her stomach and kept going down to her feet. She stammered for a moment. "I know how you feel about making me come, but—"

"Please, Malinda. I want to."

Malinda swallowed hard. As far as sex went, she preferred to give rather than receive. Hell, as far as anything went. Accepting another person's efforts overwhelmed Malinda, making her feel too exposed and filling her with squirming uncertainty about her own worthiness. In bed, this discomfort compounded with her body's sensitivity, magnifying the slightest touches until pleasure became almost agonizing. Under the best of circumstances, Malinda could barely tolerate having her cunt licked. She would much rather make Lorrie feel good, touching and teasing her body and basking in the simple joy that sensation seemed to bring to her wife.

Lately, though, Lorrie had been asking more and more frequently to go down on her. Malinda used to try to endure that when they'd first been together, but over the years, she had gotten skilled at avoiding that particular issue. Now she realized she hadn't dodged her wife's requests as smoothly as she thought. She sighed and studied the expression on Lorrie's face. Her wife was so beautiful—too beautiful for Malinda, really—and it seemed crazy to turn down her fervent wish to make Malinda come.

Still, Malinda couldn't bring herself to agree. To buy herself time, she shifted their conversation. "And you said you want to tie me up?"

Lorrie squared her shoulders. "Yes."

"That BDSM stuff has been so trendy lately," Malinda said

after a minute. "But I don't like the idea of pain. I don't want rope burn."

"Malinda." Lorrie leaned forward and took her hand. "I don't want to hurt you. I want to make you feel good, and this is the only way I could think of to get you to let me." She seemed so earnest and lovely that Malinda could not refuse.

Malinda sighed, making the sound far more theatrical than it had to be. She succeeded in winning a smile from Lorrie. "All right," Malinda said.

The smile that lit Lorrie's face made it all worth it. Lorrie gave Malinda a peck on the lips that lingered a little. She pulled her cereal bowl close again and settled into a placid chewing rhythm.

Relief flooded Malinda's body. Disaster averted. All she had to do was let her hot wife make love to her. She could manage that. Ought to be able to, anyway. She ignored the churning in her gut. She wolfed down the rest of her breakfast and promised Lorrie she'd leave work right at six so they'd have plenty of time for anniversary celebration.

"All right, where are the fuzzy handcuffs?" Malinda let the apartment door slam shut behind her.

"You're lucky I don't want to hurt you, or I'd spank you senseless for that." Lorrie came out of the bedroom, dressed in Malinda's favorite dirty-sorority-girl sweats. The back of the pants actually said JUICY. The word always made Malinda laugh—and grab Lorrie's luscious ass.

"Oooh, threatening."

In response, Lorrie narrowed her eyes in her cute-angry way, which meant she actually felt affectionate. This was a good start. A giddy good mood began to settle over Malinda. Come to think of it, she liked staying in for their anniversary. It would be good to have sex before she felt sleepy. She'd also be spared the belly full of rich French food that inevitably made her want to lie flat on her back, robbed of the energy necessary to grope her wife.

"So, seriously, where do you want me?" Malinda backed against the wall and mimed hanging from chains. She knew she was being a bit of a jerk, but not knowing what Lorrie planned had kept her keyed up all day.

"You've really got an attitude, you know that?"

The word *attitude* set off Malinda's deepest sense of rebellion. She'd heard that way too much in public school, from teachers who couldn't seem to understand what a girl went through as an out lesbian tenth-grader. She lifted her chin. "What are you going to do about it?"

"You are a terrible brat! Probably because I promised not to spank you." Lorrie sounded as if she were scolding a pet.

The tone reminded Malinda of the silliness of this whole idea. She let her body relax as Lorrie pulled her wrists off the wall. In fact, she could play with this a little more. She stuck her tongue out at Lorrie, half in jest and half from genuine childish irritation.

Lorrie gave a dramatic gasp. "Come into the bedroom. You're lucky I'm creative enough to know how to punish you without hurting you."

Malinda didn't help—Lorrie had to drag her. Malinda tried a full-on raspberry. Lorrie just grinned and shook her head. She seemed genuinely indulgent, unflappable in a way Malinda had never seen.

Malinda blinked in wonder and tried the raspberry again.

Lorrie clucked her tongue. "You're going to have to take off your clothes, Malinda, whether you like it or not."

Now that they'd reached the bedroom, Malinda glanced

toward the bed. Bright construction paper chains looped all four of the bedposts. Lorrie had pasted a red paper heart above the bed and replaced the lampshades with waxed paper fashioned into fake stained glass. She'd made it up with their nicest sheets—the ultrahigh-thread-count ones they hadn't really expected to receive from the wedding registry. It was all so cute and sweet that Malinda couldn't help but get a little more obedient. She undid the buttons down the front of her work shirt, then stepped out of her jeans.

"Take it all off," Lorrie said.

Malinda rolled her shoulders back and reached behind herself to undo her bra. "I don't see any fuzzy handcuffs."

"You really seem to want those," Lorrie teased.

"I'm just surprised."

Lorrie shrugged. "The traditional first anniversary gift is paper."

"It looks great, but I don't think it's going to hold me very long if you make me struggle."

A surprisingly wicked gleam came into Lorrie's eyes. "If you break my pretty paper chains, Malinda, I'm going to have to punish you." She sounded like a demented kindergarten teacher.

"I seriously do not want to be spanked."

Lorrie cocked her head to one side. "You really seem to lack imagination about this, Malinda. Lie down."

Malinda lay down.

"Spread out wide for me."

Malinda did. The paper chains rustled as Lorrie looped them around Malinda's arms and legs. She pulled them tighter than Malinda expected, leaving very little leeway for Malinda to move without ripping them.

"Good." Lorrie dropped her voice to a husky whisper. "Now don't move a muscle."

"What are you—Oh god..." Before Malinda had time to finish her question, Lorrie jumped onto the bed on all fours and lowered her mouth to Malinda's clit. "Lorrie, please," she hissed. "It's too much."

Lorrie slipped her index finger inside her and looked up with that innocent expression again. "You let me do it when we first met." She executed a long lick, from the top of Malinda's vulva, through the folds, over her hole and practically down to her asshole.

It felt like heaven—but not in any warm and fuzzy sense. Lorrie's tongue was hot, white light with the power to blind and burn.

"Holy Christ, Lorrie, I can't take this." Malinda clenched her fists tight, tensing every muscle in her arms to hold them still.

"Well, if you really can't, you can say 'safeword,' and I'll stop."

Lorrie swirled a circle around the shaft of Malinda's clit. Malinda gave a strangled cry. Lorrie propped her elbows on Malinda's upper thighs and pulled the hood off Malinda's clit.

Malinda couldn't even handle the sensation of air across the bared nub of flesh. When Lorrie tapped her tongue straight onto it, Malinda screamed and kicked her left leg hard.

She tore the chains around that leg clear in half.

At the sound of ripping paper, Lorrie froze and sat back on her heels. "Oh, Malinda, that's going to be very bad for you."

"What? What are you talking about?"

"Punishment."

"Listen, Lorrie, why don't you let me eat you instead? I'll happily go down on you for hours, just..."

Lorrie's index finger drove into Malinda's ribs, transforming her words into a gasping, shrieking laugh. "That tickles!"

"Yeah. That's the point." Lorrie jabbed and prodded just under Malinda's flopping breasts. Until that moment, Malinda hadn't realized the power of Lorrie's position above her. Lorrie pinned her to the bed completely, wrapping her legs around Malinda's thighs to seal herself in place.

"You need to relax, Malinda. You say you want to have fun, but how much fun have we been having? I'm not asking you to do more and more for me until you make yourself crazy. You're doing that yourself and acting like I'm the one responsible." She pressed writhing, undulating fingers into Malinda's armpits.

Malinda jerked, but knew better than to rip any more of the paper chains if she could possibly help it. She would have responded to Lorrie's words if she'd been able to speak. Instead, all she could do was pant and twitch and stare up at her beautiful wife.

"I get to punish you now, Malinda," Lorrie continued, "and this is what you get. You're going to have to laugh. Hard. Harder than you can stand it. Every time you break one of my chains, I'm going to make you laugh even more. And when you've laughed so hard that you're too exhausted to fight me, then I'm going to go down on you until I make you come. I can't make you take my love, but I can make you take that. And you're damn well going to."

Lorrie's words shocked Malinda, but her merciless, tickling hands left no way to express the feeling. Malinda struggled for breath, the laughter starting to become pain. The more she jerked beneath Lorrie, the more aware she felt of both their bodies. She'd always thought of tickling as a child's game, but now, when each spasm Lorrie forced seemed to travel straight to her cunt, it became a very adult pastime indeed.

Her wife let up for a moment and spoke in a more normal tone of voice. "I'm about to tickle you into the next dimension, bratty Malinda," she said. "Are you going to say 'safeword' or are you going to take it like a woman?"

Later, Malinda would think over all the things Lorrie had said. Now, she lifted her chin, that sense of rebellion filling her again. Slowly and very deliberately, she lifted her right arm and ripped up more of Lorrie's paper chains.

"Oh, you are asking for it." Lorrie flung her full body onto Malinda. She seemed like a writhing, tickling animal. It wasn't just her fingers. She tickled also with her toes, her hair, her lips, her teeth. She grabbed Malinda everywhere, wiggling teasing touches on the insides of her elbows, along the sides of her neck and behind her knees.

For the first few seconds, it was fun to laugh wildly. Then Malinda began to feel out of control. Breath no longer reached her lungs according to a regular rhythm—it came whenever she could manage to drag it in. Her every limb flailed wildly, controlled only by Lorrie's weight on hers. She tore up all the paper chains. She kicked a heel against the bedpost. She lost all sense of time. Never had she been so completely in someone else's power. For as long as Lorrie continued, Malinda's body would be utterly at her mercy.

She begged. She bucked. Tears ran down the sides of her face. Her chest and belly ached from laughing, and yet she could not stop.

Lorrie offered no relief. Malinda had never guessed her wife possessed the capability for such focused torture. Muscles she'd never thought about began to hurt. The tops of her thighs cramped from struggling beneath Lorrie. The sides of her neck seized. She screamed, sobbed and howled.

"Please!" Malinda shrieked. "Please! Please!"

Lorrie paused. Still, Malinda could not move. She lay flat on the bed and gasped. Lorrie leaned forward and whispered in her ear, "You still owe me five more minutes. You broke every one of my paper chains."

"God no." Malinda shook her head frantically. "I can't."

"Because I'm so nice, I'll give you another way to pay me back. You can lie still like a good girl and let me lick that pussy."

"Lorrie, I can't do that either."

Lorrie tsked and shook her head sadly, then lifted her hands like claws. "I'll have to go back to tickling, then."

"Oh please, no!"

"Then lie still." Now Lorrie's voice became a sensual purr.

"All right," Malinda said. She thought she'd die if she laughed any more. She allowed herself to go limp, exhausted enough that she didn't have the energy to struggle when Lorrie applied her excruciating tongue to Malinda's slit.

Lorrie moved slower this time. Malinda panted like a marathon runner, her eyes squeezed shut, but her muscles tickled to submission. "Good," Lorrie soothed. "That's good. See, this doesn't hurt. I'm not hurting you."

"But you are," Malinda groaned. She didn't think she could explain how badly this hurt deep down in her chest, in the center of her heart. Her eyes slitted open. Beautiful Lorrie lay between Malinda's legs, with her impossibly wholesome looks, licking Malinda with a loving expression that wounded every part of her.

"Shh," Lorrie said.

She lapped Malinda gently, yet the pleasure was still just this side of bearable. Malinda stirred, about to push her head away, but Lorrie laid a cautioning hand on Malinda's stomach. She lifted her head and studied Malinda. Lorrie's fierce teasing had melted away, but Malinda had still been stripped bare by it. She lay vulnerable and defenseless before her wife, feeling more naked than she'd ever been.

Lorrie stroked Malinda's head, her fingers catching in the tangles of her black hair. She retrieved what was left of the paper chains near Malinda's left hand and draped them lightly over her wrist. "You're still tied down," she whispered. "Don't move. Don't break the chains." Lorrie repeated the gesture at each of the bed's corners, and this time Malinda didn't feel the need to tug and test.

She breathed steadily and slowly. Each of the paper chains could have weighed hundreds of pounds for how firmly they held her now. She wanted them to chain her to Lorrie forever.

"That's good," Lorrie said, her voice barely audible. "You're not going anywhere now."

And once more, her head dipped between Malinda's legs, her neck curved and gentle like a deer drinking from a pool. This time, pure ecstasy dripped into Malinda's slit along with Lorrie's saliva. Its rough surface forced pleasure into her pelvis and up into her body, warming her everywhere. Malinda realized she was crying, but, wrapped in Lorrie's paper chains, she lay still and let the tears come.

Then the sweet, stabbing joy of Lorrie's tongue pierced the last of Malinda's defenses and release came, bringing with it a cry from the depths of Malinda's soul. "Please! I can't!"

"You can," Lorrie whispered against Malinda's cunt, and there was no refuting her, because Malinda did. She came hard, held in place by Lorrie's paper chains and her love.

Lorrie remained motionless, her tongue flat against Malinda's clit, until the last of the spasms passed. Then she crawled up Malinda's body to lie at her side. Even exhausted this way, trembling with pleasure and emotion, Malinda felt compelled to ask, "What can I do for you?"

"Sh. You just did."

ROPENOSIS

Teresa Noelle Roberts

Get undressed, Diana," Michael said, caressing the hank of blue rope as he spoke. It was an invitation to delight, couched as an order I'd have a hard time questioning, and that just made it better. Easier. Even I had a hard time starting a conversation about something scientific or getting lost in a tangential train of thought when I was being "ordered" to do something I thought was a wonderful idea anyway. We hadn't been dating long. I wasn't sure Michael knew yet if I preferred beer or wine, Mexican or Chinese takeout, but he'd made a point of figuring out the important things quickly.

I shed my dress and panties as if they burned me. But while I did, I kept my eyes on his long, elegant fingers stroking the rope. He watched me as intently as I watched him and it seemed he touched my skin instead of the rope, or as if the rope and his hand already caressed me as they soon would. I was damp and pleasantly flustered before he placed himself behind me.

A length of soft rope, cooler than the warm June air, passed over the bare skin of my belly. I sighed and leaned back against him. He was shirtless but still had jeans on, and the contrasting textures of denim and furred skin, along with the texture of the rope, pushed away the day's petty concerns. "We're trying something new tonight," he purred in my ear.

"Tell me more." We were new enough together that we were still marking off shared firsts: first spanking, first rope harness, first hypnosis, first sex with me fully tied up, first (laughable) attempt at role-play. But I sensed from a hint of nervous excitement in Michael's voice that this would be a different sort of first, something neither of us had tried before.

Considering we came into the relationship with pasts that would make Nina Hartley proud, that was enough to make me both anxious and aroused.

Very aroused. What could he have in mind that would be new to both of us?

The rope brushed over my nipples, sending a shiver to my clit. "Just feel." Michael's voice dropped to a slow, seductive rumble, as close to Barry White as a white guy with a tenor voice could get. His hypnosis voice. I'd never thought of hypnosis as something sexy before Michael. But when he put me under, I could relax completely in a way that even my beloved rope couldn't allow me. So far we'd mostly used it to help me sleep, but I'd adored the couple of times he'd turned me into a helpless—but very wet and willing—doll to be posed and played with.

I had no idea what Michael had in mind now, but if it involved hypnosis *and* rope, I planned to relax and find out. After I asked one more question. "So are you going to hypnotize me first, or…?"

The rope pulled back from my skin and Michael chuckled. "You never got past the toddler 'why' stage, did you? So many questions."

"It's why I'm a good engineer."

"And why you can't sleep at night, because you're still asking the universe why at two in the morning. There's no need to ask questions now. Just follow my voice, Diana. Follow and feel."

The Barry White voice was back, and so was the rope, wrapping around my rib cage just under my breasts, guided by Michael's strong hands. "Feel the rope. This first round anchors you so you can fly safely. Feel it hold you like I hold you."

I did feel it, in a way I wouldn't normally. I mean, I *know* part of the thrill of bondage was the paradoxical way restraint freed inhibitions. But following Michael's voice, I was conscious of that sense of safety inside the edginess. Or maybe subconscious of it, like a deeper part of me was getting into the game even before wave after wave of sensation got my overly keen analytical brain to shut the fuck up.

"I'm going to put you in a chest harness and rope corset. And each time the rope wraps around your body, your busy mind is going to get quieter and you'll slip farther into hypnosis." He passed the rope around my rib cage again, snugging it in the back with a twist or knot that I couldn't be bothered to try to figure out, though I usually agonized over exactly what he was doing when I couldn't see him. Not because I thought I'd ever need to duplicate it, but because it bothered me not to know how things worked. This time, though, I could just enjoy the rope. I sighed at the way it touched and held me, at the way Michael's hands traced the rope's path on my skin. My muscles relaxed and I took a deep breath in just before Michael said, "Now take a deep breath in...and when you let it out, send your worries and concerns with it."

I hadn't thought I was worried about anything, precisely, just ruminating now and then over the prototype sitting in my lab at work.

But when I let that breath out, tension fled that I hadn't known I was holding. I hadn't realized that deep down I felt like I should be working on that prototype instead of playing with Michael, even though it was Saturday night and I'd worked until three that afternoon.

But what if I had an idea and I was tied up and half out of my mind?

He wrapped the rope again, this time above my breasts. "Feel the rope taking control of your body, Diana. Feel it taking control of your mind. All your wonderful ideas will still be there when you come back. They'll even be clearer because you've given them a chance to rest and grow."

For a guy I'd known only a few months, Michael understood me too damn well. Then again, he was a scientist himself, so he got how I'd become trapped in a quest for answers.

"But what if...?"

He laid one long-fingered hand over my lips. The hand still held a rope end, and the length of rope brushing my torso as he moved his hand silenced me as if it had brushed the question away. "If something that might be important pops into your head, imagine it being saved to a file for later, and the file is getting backed up in the cloud so you can access it wherever you are. Just let those thoughts be saved in your backup file while you enjoy the moment." I nodded slowly. The metaphor worked for me, better than the more abstract ones he'd tried during other hypnosis sessions.

"Good girl. Feel the rope. As the rope touches you, you'll let go a little more." He continued to wrap me as he spoke. "Feel the rope. Feel my hands. Feel them pushing the nagging thoughts out of your brain and pushing anything you might need later into a file for safekeeping." His deep, low voice compelled me, and the rope moving over my skin soothed me. "You'll slip deeper into hypnosis, deeper into pleasure, whenever more rope touches you." As he brought the rope over one shoulder and between my breasts, drawing the two bands of rope together, I stopped trying to track what he was doing. Normally I'd have a mental soundtrack of *Now he's doing X*, but instead I let myself sink into the soothing sensation of rope and hands on my skin.

He finished the harness, tying it off in the back with a decisiveness that somehow deepened my blissed-out state. "Now I'm making the corset," he whispered. "And with each coil going down your torso, you'll drop a little deeper. When I'm done—when I tie off the ends—you will be unable to do anything except feel and enjoy. And then you'll come for me."

I clenched at those words, at the surety in his voice. He was confident I'd obey, that I'd come, and in that moment, so was I. No questioning how I could come without him touching my clit. I just knew I would.

He began to make the rope corset, winding down, tying off after each coil, and with each coil, telling me I was sinking deeper into hypnosis, deeper into a place with no thoughts, only sensations.

Between arousal, rope on my skin and his hypnotic persuasions, I was already dreamy and unable to think clearly. By the time he'd made three wraps, my mind felt full of honey, and empty of anything but that delicious slow sweetness and an aching arousal. I couldn't have solved for *X* if my life depended on it.

For a second, I became aware of my slow thoughts, my nearly empty mind, and froze in panic. "Feel," Michael said, simply. "Let go and feel. Don't fight it."

I took a deep breath and let the panic go and felt myself sinking into a soft, blissful place where nothing mattered but me and Michael and the rope on my sensitive skin.

He kissed me, a leisurely, sweet-hot kiss to match my syrupy thoughts, and I found myself relaxing into the kiss in a way I normally couldn't, simply enjoying his lips, his tongue, his arms around me, and not thinking about what had happened before, might happen next, was going on in the lab or in some rival lab in Japan.

I kissed, and for that moment, that was all I did.

My body blossomed. I'd been wet and aroused before, but now I was all floaty arousal, and it was all centered in my lips and tongue. The arousal filled me to the point where I trembled on the verge of orgasm before Michael broke the kiss and went back to wrapping me in rope.

He was almost done. Only a few more wraps around my hips. How many I couldn't say, because counting was too much work. He passed the two ends of the rope between my legs, first one, then the other tugging against my cunt lips, pulling them open as Michael move the ends of the rope into the back of the corset.

I only know that was what he was doing because he'd done the rope corset thing before and I'd made mental notes the whole time. But while it was going on this time, I wasn't thinking of anything except how the ropes embraced and caressed me, how hot my cunt was, how swollen my clit, and even those weren't exactly thoughts in the usual sense. No logic, no analysis, certainly no questions or distractions. Barely even words, just glorious sensations overwhelming my body and my honey-filled brain. I was trembling and moaning without language, thrusting my hips back at Michael, thrusting them forward at the air in search of an invisible lover.

But I didn't beg for mercy, didn't ask for a direct touch on my throbbing clit, because it didn't occur to me that there was more beyond this everlasting moment of sweet need. I was in the moment, and the moment was in Michael's hands, in Michael's control. He would take care of me. I wasn't thinking enough to articulate that.

I simply knew. I trusted. I waited.

When he finished weaving the rope ends into the back of the corset, he pulled me close against his body, and said, "Come, Diana."

I came.

As simple as that, and as complicated. He said *come* and I spiraled down into dark pleasure and then rocketed out of the darkness screaming and shaking, seeing fire behind my eyes and feeling miraculous fire coursing through my whole body.

The fire burned away some of my trance, cleared some of the syrup in my brain, and when I calmed a little, I managed to ask a couple of questions, even if I sounded about as insightful and clever as a fluffy Persian kitten granted a human voice. "Wow. How did you learn to do that? And what can I do for you?"

"Drop deeper," he whispered, leading me to the bed. "No questions yet. Just pleasure."

It was the next morning before I asked another question, and that was, "Want to go out for breakfast? You'll need to untie me first."

Michael decided on breakfast in bed.

I, ROBOT

Heidi Champa

S o, this is why you're late for dinner, again."

He looked up at me with guilt in his eyes. His giant, magnifying-goggle-covered eyes. The circuit board in front of him was half together and the soldering iron in his hands was still smoking. His radio was playing some crazy hip-hop and the clock on the wall was all the evidence I needed that he had blown me off for the robots yet again. I had gotten dressed up in my favorite outfit, right down to the new stilettos I'd bought especially for the night. Well, maybe not exactly for the dinner, but they worked nonetheless. I looked hot and he was still in his ratty work clothes right down to the tattered lab coat he wore all the time. I glared at him, but his sheepish grin made it difficult to stay as mad as I would have liked.

"I can explain."

"Save your breath, Casey. I'm not in the mood to hear the latest in a long line of bullshit. I guess I'll just have to accept that your work will always come first."

"That's not true, Dana, and you know it."

"Really? Because here we are in your lab when we're supposed to be at a fancy dinner. Oh and why are we going to that fancy dinner? Because you ditched me last week for your stupid project and you promised to make it up to me. Tonight!"

He stood and held his hands up in surrender. When he came toward me, I took a step back, ready to bolt out the door and head home to the comfort of my couch. The shoes, while hot, were starting to make my feet hurt.

"I know I fucked up. But I swear I have a very good reason. If you'll give me a chance, I can explain."

"Fine. Go ahead and explain. I can't wait to hear this."

He led me over to a table where two robot arms were attached to a huge contraption made of metal and plastic and god knows what else. I had absolutely no idea what I was looking at, but Casey's mechanical brain always impressed me.

"I thought you were going to explain, Casey."

"I thought it might be easier to just show you."

He started typing on a beat-up laptop and right before my eyes, the two robot arms sprang to life, lifting up and moving around in a stiff mimic of human motion.

"Holy shit, that's so cool."

"I know. We just got them to really work tonight. And I was so pumped, I didn't want to stop. Do you understand?"

I watched the arms move toward me and retreat, the long, slim, metal-jointed fingers drumming on an invisible keyboard. I turned and looked at Casey and let him wrap his arms around me.

"I guess. I'm still pissed though. Even though you're freaking brilliant and awesome."

"That's a start. I suppose I'll just have to make things up to you twice tonight."

His eyebrow rose in a sweetly familiar way, and I melted a bit in his strong arms.

"What did you have in mind, Casey?"

He spun me around so I was facing the table again. The robot arms started to move until one of them was right in front of me.

"Don't be so shy, Dana. Say hello."

It felt ridiculous, but I reached out and shook hands with the robot. Then it was on to the double high five. I couldn't stop laughing as the robot mirrored my movements, but the giggles died when the mechanical arms grabbed me tight around the wrists.

"What the fuck, Casey? Make it let me go."

"Does it hurt?"

"No, but—"

The fake hands squeezed me a bit tighter and started pulling away, forcing me to lean over the table. They stopped just as my face was inches away from the wood surface, my feet struggling to stay on the ground.

"This isn't funny, Casey. Do whatever you have to do and make it stop."

"I have a better idea."

Instead of releasing me, Casey ran a hand over my ass, inching up the fabric of my pencil skirt. I felt the cool air of the lab flowing over my skin as he exposed me, my thong the only thing between us. His calloused fingers teased my skin, raising goose bumps. A few playful slaps followed, and I couldn't keep quiet any longer.

"What the fuck are you doing?"

"Making it up to you, like I said."

"This is your idea of making it up to me?"

"Yup."

A few seconds passed before I felt his hands on my hips and my thong start to slide down my legs and off my feet. With a hand around each ankle, he urged my legs wide. I struggled against the hard metal bonds around my wrists, even though I knew it was pointless. All I could do was stare at the wall, which was littered with coiled wires, pliers and various things that I couldn't name. My eyes fell closed when his fingers started dancing up the backs of my legs, half tickling and half caressing.

I moved, trying to get away from his touch, but it was no use. I was trapped, which was obviously exactly what he wanted.

"Casey…"

"Just relax, babe. I promise, by the time I'm done, you'll forget all about me being late again."

I opened my mouth to protest some more, but the words died in my throat when his tongue started tracing meandering lines across the back of my thigh. His fingers dug into my flesh, his grip nearly as strong as the robot's. His mouth eased closer and closer to my already damp pussy, but stayed far enough away to leave me wanting.

"Casey, quit messing around."

"My, my. So impatient, Dana."

"What exactly did you expect?"

"Exactly this. Don't worry, I won't make you wait too much longer, but come on, I have to have a little fun."

"What about my fun?"

"Just getting to that."

A single finger ran from the pucker of my ass down the split of my pussy lips, sliding over my wetness until he came to rest on my clit. I gasped against the wood table, my arms straining against the robot's literal iron grip. Casey started to trace small circles, first one way and then the other until I could barely stand it. Suddenly his finger was gone from my clit and slipped inside me with no resistance at all. Slowly, so damn slowly, he moved in and out of me, finger-fucking my pussy until I was nearly panting.

"God, you're so hot when you're excited, Dana."

I didn't know if he wanted an answer, but I was too focused on the feelings to give one. All I could do was moan as his invading digits moved within me, the walls of my pussy grasping him tight. I pushed back against him, as much as my robot restraints would allow, urging him to move faster. He didn't oblige, but he did add another finger to my cunt, stretching me open a little farther.

"Casey, please."

"That's what I like to hear. Say please again."

I groaned and bit my lip, my thighs beginning to tremble as he entered me again and again.

"Please...you're driving me crazy."

"And here I thought I only did that when I stood you up for dinner."

"I want you inside me, Casey. I don't know how much longer I can wait."

"Well, let's see how much longer, shall we?"

The whimper came out of my mouth before I could stop it, and I was sure it was exactly what Casey wanted to hear. His fingers were gone from my cunt but were soon replaced by the swirling power of his tongue. Casey gripped my thighs as he licked and sucked my clit, making me buck back against him. My wrists were starting to hurt from straining against the robot's grip, but the little bites of pain only made the whole thing more exciting. I looked up at the towering apparatus that held me so tight and cried out as Casey slapped his palm against my ass. My nipples were straining against the lace bra I'd chosen with

this type of thing in mind. Well, maybe not this type of thing
exactly. Just when I thought I was going to explode, everything
stopped. I heard Casey's shuffling feet behind me, the sound
getting quieter. My panic made me yell out, even though I knew
it wouldn't do any good.

"Hey, where the hell are you going? You can't leave me like
this."

When he returned, he slapped my ass again, laughing at
me.

"Patience my dear."

"I'm out of patience."

"Just a little bit more."

I pulled at the robot hands, wishing I could tear the whole
thing down, just so I could get my hands on Casey. But I knew
it was futile. When his hands were back on me, I settled down
a bit, but I was desperate by this point. The head of his cock
came to rest at my wet opening, and I immediately pushed back
against him. He stayed far enough away that I could only feel
the slightest brush of him.

"Fuck me, Casey. Fuck me now."

He leaned over me and whispered right in my ear.

"If you insist."

The last word was punctuated by the thrust of his hips and
he was buried in me to the hilt. He fucked me slow and hard,
his whole body pressed against mine. His voice was once again
in my ear, throwing gasoline on my fire.

"I haven't been able to stop thinking about this moment. I
knew you'd show up when I was late. This was the first thing I
wanted my bionic hands to do."

"Wouldn't rope have been cheaper?"

"But not nearly as fun."

My feet started to slip as he fucked me faster; the gorgeous heels had little effect on the concrete floor. My wrists were aching to be released, almost as much as I was. Casey reached underneath me and played with my clit, nuzzling his lips against the back of my neck. I couldn't hold back any longer, my body too tense for too long. I was coming harder than I had in forever, my whole body racked with the pleasure Casey had denied me for long torturous minutes. He soon followed, groaning loudly in my ear as he came, his thrusts stuttering to a halt.

Everything was quiet in the lab, except for the ticking of the large clock on the wall. Casey pulled away from me, and I heard his fingers racing over the keys of his laptop. With a high-pitched whine, the robot hands moved again, slowly opening and letting me free. I stood up on wobbly feet letting my skirt fall down my hips. My thong was a few feet away, crumbled in a little ball. I picked it up and slipped it on, catching my reflection in a cracked mirror on the wall. My lipstick was smudged and my mascara had run. My hair was disheveled and not in a cute way. I could only laugh as Casey came up behind me and wrapped me in his arms.

"How are your wrists?"

"A little sore. But nothing I can't handle."

"So, tell me, Dana. Am I forgiven?"

I turned and kissed him as he eased his lab coat off his shoulders. I watched as he turned off the light and put his robot arms to bed for the night. I ran my hand down one long metal bar that made up its forearm.

"Do you mind if we stop at home before dinner, Casey?" I asked.

"Oh, come on, I think you look great, but if you insist," he said with a grin.

I looked down at my disheveled outfit and smiled.

"Not exactly the look I was going for when I left the house tonight."

He slipped his hand in mine as we walked toward the door.

"So, you never answered me, Dana. Am I forgiven?" he asked, even though he already knew the answer.

"That depends," I said.

"Depends on what?"

"On how long you make me wait to come back to the lab."

MAGIC BOOTS

Amy Dillon

The boots are the center of Noah's fantasy—and therefore, mine.

But I think maybe they worked a little magic on me, too. I'm not quite the foot freak he is...but after a month with my boots, I'm getting there. And once I see how Noah reacts to my magic boots? I think I might be a little bit of a *convert*.

Noah doesn't know I've got these particular boots. Not yet. That's what makes them hot.

But *I* know. I know everything about them. I know how they feel on my feet, and I know how they feel in my face. I know how their subtle contours feel against my tongue, how the smell intoxicates me. And I'm not even a foot freak, really. I just like to turn my husband on. And from the way I've so easily trained myself to get dizzy just from thinking about these boots, I'm pretty sure Noah's going to like them. He and I tend to have tastes in common. And if there's one thing I'm confident we'll agree on, it's that I look *hot* in these boots.

The buttery leather molds to my calves, displaying just the right amount of their shape along with the rigid perfection that spells a well-constructed boot. The soft, supple feel of the material seems to radiate sex, both in touch and in scent, when you get up close and personal with them. I've kissed them as often as Noah is going to. Or at least I gave them a very good introduction to how it feels to be kissed by a horny human tongue. I think they like it.

I first saw them a month ago. Noah coveted them in the store. On one of our rare trips into the City, we had stopped at this specialty boot store and Noah just about lost it over these. I teased him about them at the time. I played with him later a little, joking about them. Then I dropped it. They were too expensive, we agreed. Far too frivolous. Not at all practical. I could easily be Noah's "Mistress," even without a pair of really hot boots, right? And I am, I guess, sort of part-time, when it suits my fancy and his, which is not as often as I'd like.

But that's going to change, because I've been practicing. I went back and bought the boots, in secret. I've been wearing them. I've been wearing them a lot. And believe me, I've had a hell of a time hiding them from him. I almost can't believe he hasn't smelled them. I feel like I can smell them all the way down the block. And it makes me wet.

But I want to surprise him—and I'm not really ready to surprise Noah with his fantasy boots until I'm ready to *sell them*. And to sell them, I need to know them. So I've worn them for the last month...whenever I could. At first, I told myself I needed to "break them in," but realistically that didn't seem necessary, since the soft, supple leather molded to my feet like they were made for them. The whisper of a blister I got on my left big toe was the only hint that they needed to be "broken." Maybe it was me that needed to be broken, if you know what I mean.

Now, I just admit that I kept putting them on and wearing them whenever Noah wasn't around because I wanted to know how it felt to wear them...not physically (that feels *fucking awesome*) but *emotionally*.

See, there's something special about these boots. They're magic. The way they look on me, and the way I feel in them, tells me just how important and powerful I am. And that's sexy as hell.

If I'm seriously going to dominate my husband—and I plan to—then I've got to feel good about how I look in boots, right?

But it wasn't easy. I would wear them around the house, and get so comfortable in them. It's not that I would forget I had them on—no, that seems almost impossible. I'd just get so damned *turned on*. I'd be doing household tasks or just kicking back and reading, or whatever. I'd get really turned on and I'd have to fool around a little bit. With myself, I mean. Not the goal-oriented kind of fooling around...just the *yeah, this is good* kind of fooling. I'd get lost in the pleasure of touching myself, feeling them on me, thinking about all the things I would do to Noah when I granted him his fantasy.

The son of a bitch almost spoiled it. He almost caught me *twice*. I would get so distracted by touching myself that I wouldn't hear him come home, or wouldn't realize he was awake. Twice just this past week, as the anticipation drove me crazy and I got more excited and bold about wearing my boots, he almost caught me in them. That would have ruined everything, wouldn't it?

But both times, I managed to evade him and hide them— once under the bathroom sink, once under the bed—where they could later be retrieved and returned to their hiding place at the top of the closet.

I got to know my boots pretty well. I got to know how good

it feels to wear them, especially when I'm not wearing anything else. It's a really strange feeling to be naked in boots. It took me a while to take myself seriously in them. The first few times, I had to wear a bra and panties. I tried them with a garter belt and stockings, but it seemed like kind of a mixed metaphor.

Finally I would wear them with shorts and a tank top, around the house, feeling the pleasure of their weighty power on my feet and tight around my calves. I started to regularly polish my boots, buff them, caress them, smell them. It became exquisitely natural to feel their supple touch against my finger-tips. I became more and more comfortable with the pleasure of the boots on my feet. I would kick cabinets closed just to feel the power of my boots against them. Then I'd toe the cabinets open again. I'd climb stairs just to climb them. I'd gotten mild blisters the first few times I wore them, but those had vanished long before I'd gotten comfortable taking off the tank top...let alone the shorts. But that happened, too. I finally got the hang of walking around nude in my boots. My heart would pound, at first. I was afraid to look at myself in the mirror, for fear I'd look silly. I did, the first few times. Before long, I realized that I didn't look silly at all. I looked *hot*.

I can't be sure what changed. At some point in the last month, the power of the boots just sort of seeped into my body...and my soul. In that wonderful month, as Noah and I were having truly magnificent sex—probably because I've been in a state of constant arousal—the power of my pussy and the power of my boots just melded together and turned me into some kind of weird hybrid superhero.

Now the boots feel so exquisitely natural on me. And they feel far more natural when I'm naked.

I'm glad for the times I hid them from Noah, wore them when he was asleep or not around, all the times I touched myself wearing them, feeling their power and their scent suffuse my sex. It helped me learn just how perfect they were for me, and it made me perfect for them.

And it was worth it. When Noah walks in the door, he just about loses it.

He finds me in my "throne," wearing nothing but the boots. Most days, most nights, this is my favorite armchair, a big cushy thrift-store monstrosity with a hideous green checkered pattern, tilted at just the angle at which I love to loaf. It emits the faint aroma of incense and weed from my stoner roommates three houses back, before I even met Noah or ever knew I'd need my "throne" to be my *throne*. I always called it my "throne," as a joke, and that's why Noah finds me there.

It isn't a joke anymore.

Tonight, my throne has a black silk sheet over it, because I don't want candle wax on my favorite chair. And a few other things are already dripping, if you catch my meaning. I'm naked except for my knee-high boots, and I'm so turned on I could scream.

The front door opens, and Noah sees me. He's got our mail clutched in his teeth like a dog. His eyes go wide. His jaw drops. Mail flutters everywhere. His briefcase slips from his grasp. It hits the floor with a *thunk*. Noah stands there, staring.

I'm stark-raving naked except for these beautiful, glorious boots. Of course, I've got makeup on, and these trashy hoop earrings Noah inexplicably loves. I've got a bracelet or two and my wedding ring. And I've got a faint dusting of body glitter across my breasts; with the way I've cocked the carefully cali-brated lights at just the angle to accent the tone of my flesh, the glitter really makes my skin "pop," and I mean that in a good way. But what it really does is make the boots seem even more supple and shiny. Since I've just finished polishing them, I know they're at their best.

I'm sprawled, as if he caught me in a casual, relaxed moment, which he didn't. I'm on pins and needles, but the sprawl is important to the tableau. One leg is down, one boot on the floor. The other dangles in midair, as I've tossed it over the black-shrouded arm of my throne, my leg bent casually at the knee.

That means my legs are spread, my hips raised a little, my sex open and visible to my husband.

And anyone else out there who happens to walk down the street.

"Close the door, will you? The cat might get out. And I think there are better ways to meet the neighbors."

I'm amazed at how confident and calm my voice sounds. Even making a sarcastic crack, I've got that sonorous purr that I've practiced for weeks, always while wearing the boots.

Noah's eyes are all over me, his tongue lolling out. He's practically drooling. He fumbles his wingtip back and kicks the door closed.

"You went back and bought them," he said.

"Yes," I say. "Get over here and show me how grateful you are."

That voice again—irresistible, hypnotic. It seems to emanate from the power in my feet. Maybe the voice is theirs, not mine. Maybe it's they who stop Noah dead in his tracks as he crosses the living room from the front door, making it halfway to my throne before my hand comes up with the supple black rod aimed at his face.

It's one of those toys we've played with, but he could never handle it for very long. Or maybe I could never handle it. It's a very heavy pain toy—a weighty, flexible rod that snaps like a bitch and sends an agonizing thud through the victim's body. We tried it a couple of times. Noah said he liked it; he likes heavier pain than I've ever given him before. I know that should be enough, but I'm just not that nasty a bitch, you know? My nerves get a little ragged when I hurt him. Noah screamed like a girl when I smacked him with it. I felt terrible and haven't been able to use it again.

Something tells me I'll use it tonight.

More importantly, the black rod is a kind of totem, like the boots. As soon as Noah sees it, he knows I'm serious.

"Uh-uh," I say. "Have you forgotten your place?" *That voice again—it's magic.* "How does a husband greet his wife?"

A shiver goes through Noah's body. He shrugs, and his suit coat goes sliding down his arms and falls to the hardwood floor. His dress shirt joins it. His pants go next, and then his undershirt. At some point he's kicked off his wingtips, but by then I'm fully distracted as I lower my left leg and situate the boots where they belong—sturdily on the ground, twelve inches apart.

Noah, still kicking off his socks, drops to his knees and putts his mouth up against them. "Wait," I tell him. Noah looks up from my boots, eyes frightened, mouth wet with spittle. As he watches, my hand dips down beside my throne. It comes up dangling a heavy strip of leather, studded with chrome. From its clasp, there depends a padlock.

"Show me your throat," I tell him.

He obeys me, tipping his head back so I can secure the collar around his neck. His breath comes tight and hard to his spit-wet lips. I clasp the collar and close the lock. The padlock's mechanism is stiff; it has never been used. I press it tightly together, and it closes with a sharp clicking sound.

I push Noah's head back down.

"Now you can say 'Hello,'" I tell him.

Noah's mouth presses to the supple leather again, and he begins to kiss it. Seeing him worship those boots sends a charge through me. I feel the pressure of his tongue against my instep, against my calf, against my knee. He licks up to my thigh, and starts kissing his way up toward my pussy, drawing a deep breath of my scent.

I push him back down with the tip of the rod.

"When you've earned it," I tell him.

I can see the shadow of his cock, stiffening between his bare thighs.

I guide him back down to my magic boots. His mouth molds to the leather again. I caress my husband's back and head with my hand and with the tip of the black rod, reminding him what's to come if he doesn't satisfy me—satisfy *them*. Reminding him what he'll face if he fails to pay the proper obeisance to my magic boots.

But that's not going to happen, because he's worshipping them as if it's all he was made for. He kisses; he suckles; he licks. He caresses them lightly with his fingertips, and gently strokes my calves as he bends down low to lick the arches, the tips, even the soles.

My husband makes love to my boots with a heartbreaking tenderness. I watch him intently, feeling the erotic power coursing through me.

My pleasure mounts higher with each wet, drooling kiss he gives my magic boots.

It isn't long before he's earned the right to lick higher, worshipping my pussy—and that's when the fun really begins.

My magic boots demand obedience, and they always get what they want.

Luckily for me, my magic boots love to share.

ONE ROPE

Graydancer

I am the rope that binds.

Every time he picks me up, I wonder if he'll be able to control me. It's not that I don't want to help; I don't want, period. I'm a rope. I have no feelings except those that are put into me. Frustration. Admiration. Lust. But we've been together a long time, he and I, and sometimes the magic happens, and sometimes it doesn't. Lately, it does, more often than not—especially with this woman who sits in *seiza* before us. I wonder, idly, if this will be one of those special times when his will and her passion transform me from this cold coil into a warm, tangled, sweaty mess on the floor.

Time will tell. He stands behind her, somewhere between protective and predatory. I feel him take me up, fingers confidently finding a tiny loop, and with a sure flick of his wrist he releases me. I fly out across the smooth tatami mat, a loop falling across her upper thigh gracefully bared under the hem of the silk kimono. She tenses, slightly, under me. It changes to a subtle shudder as he draws me across her skin, warming my fibers measure by deliberate measure. His eyes are not on me; they focus on her body, noticing this beautiful anxious anticipation as I move across her. Her breathing deepens, her eyes flicker up to his, then down again, coy but eager.

His eyes are present. No thought of future, or of past, here in this moment with me, with her, and that awareness strengthens the will that I feel coursing through his hands. I catch a glimpse, as he draws my doubled lengths through strong fingers, of what he intends to do. How he will connect to her through me.

This is going to be one of the tangled, sweaty times. I can tell.

Finally his hands reach my end, two tiny knots, my entire length slightly warm from my journey across her flesh and through his grip. He reaches back to my midpoint, where I fold over, and holds that loop as he stretches me taut between his clenched fists, slowly pulling me wider until his arms can pass over her head. She watches me as my line passes down in front of her line of sight, and licks her lips in anticipation. She wants me. She wants me on her skin again, tight, holding her, caressing her, hurting her. But I can do nothing, until he does it to me.

There is a pause, pregnant with his intention and her anticipation. Then he moves. He presses the length of me painfully tight across the kimono, digging into the upper swell of her breasts. I can feel the expanse of smooth silk interrupted by her hot flesh exposed at the collar. He pulls harder drawing her whole body back against him, and I feel her heartbeat accelerating. She is caught between the unforgiving painful line of me and the heat of his muscled chest. We hold her tight between us for a moment, ensnared by rope and man. Her breath catches a bit, then steadies as we wait.

Then he moves quickly, a hand pulling my running end through the bight behind her back so I encircle her completely.

I hold her closer as he pulls tighter, feeling her body tense and then surrender into my embrace. I am not vicious, I do not clench. I am soft, adjusting to her smooth curves under the silk. But I am also relentless. As long as he holds my ends tight I will not release her.

He pulls harder and I squeeze, biting into her arms. She moans and he smiles. He loosens me slightly and again my embrace is soft and secure. He draws the length of me up, over her shoulder and down again between her breasts. Like our first lay he draws this fast behind her body, his chest pushing harder against her back, and now I am the one sandwiched between them. I can feel both their hearts beating strong and quick with the passion we now share. The sexual connection charges through me as he loops and twists me tight across her torso again, encircling her breasts and traveling down. I run tight down her soft belly, feeling it tremble with constricted breath as I am drawn tight.

As he winds me around, I stroke her with every slight exploration as she feels the limits of the cage he has created out of me. She stretches an arm, pushes a leg out, but I am firm. If he were less skilled, less pure of purpose, I would let her go, let her find the tiny niches such sloppy rope work inadvertently leaves.

But not this time. His desire was that she be bound, and I am the instrument of his will. Still holding my ends in one hand, he pulls me tighter across the kimono, roughly opening it in places so that it is no longer a barrier to her flesh. Her breast is exposed, then the other, skin flushed as they push between my wraps, each tipped by a rippled cone of pink desire. He adjusts me slightly and now I can rub rough against that pinkness, listening as she makes keening sounds of desire, every breath pushing her flesh harder against me.

He shifts suddenly, gripping her upper arm and pulling her sideways. She cries out, unable to catch herself as she falls the

short distance toward the mat, arms tight in my loops. We catch
her instead, his fist anchoring me as I hold her torso hovering
inches from the floor. I am looped rather than knotted and
gravity squeezes me tighter, holding her breathless just inches
from the floor.

We wait to feel her surrender, that moment when her body
relaxes into helpless trust of his skill and my strength. Then
he gently lowers us to the mat. As she lies on her side the short
kimono rides up higher on her thigh.

The exposed skin seems to inflame him, and suddenly I am
again moving quickly under his hand, unwrapping one length,
two, her breath releasing with gasping cries as he draws her
leg in and winds me tight around shin and thigh. I creak as he
cinches me in against myself, her bound leg drawn up against
her chest. I hold her there, unrelenting, as his free hand flips the
ends of the kimono open. His nostrils flare as the aroma of her
engorged sex fills the room, and I feel his grip tighten.

With a quick jerk he pulls me tighter, lifting up her hips. He
slaps her cunt with an open hand, the wet cracking sound rever-
berating through the length of me still taut between her body
and his fist. She cries out at the impact, but as I hold her exposed
I feel her hips lift higher. She craves the sensation, wants more
against her clit and mons. His next slap, and the next, bring
more heat to her core, and I feel a slight trembling aftershock
from each blow slowly building throughout her body. His eyes
are focused with sensuous cruelty on the soundless ecstatic O
of her mouth.

He pauses, letting a bit of slack into me, and I feel the shudder
go through her entire body with each throbbing breath. A deep
moan comes from her center, trailing into a whine of need. She
and I are both charged through every wrap and twist of fiber
and flesh with the burning lustful need to cum. Knowing his

tastes, I wonder if he will let her. He is sometimes mercifully generous, delivering orgasm after orgasm to the ones I bind, and sometimes he deliberately withholds that release. There is a certain piquant satisfaction to that starved desire, knowing that later the woman will furiously rub one out while lost in the memory of my harsh touch drawn by him on her skin.

But now his hands move, one drawing her leg open while the other pulls me deliciously through the luscious wet folds between her legs. The electric charge of pleasure surges through us both as her juices cover me. I swell and soak them in.

This is different. This is not what he usually does, when we play together with his willing prey. I realize that my world has changed, because I am no longer his. Her body's desire has covered me, and that means I will never tie anyone else. I am bound to her permanently, and that makes this moment of crushing passion all the sweeter.

He draws me tight up behind her and I dig deeper, pressing through the soft curls of her mons hard against her pubic bone. My twin strands lie like electrified steel just to the left of her throbbing clit before driving down into the sweet, hot, juicy cleft labia. Deeper down I press roughly against the tender rosebud of her ass as he pulls my knotted ends hard. The tension lifts her ass slightly from the tightly woven tatami. Her hips grind against me, frantic, transforming friction to pleasure in an alchemy of lust and pain. She presses harder. His grip is firm as she dashes her need against my Charybdisiac bonds. He is motionless, caught in the present, touching her whole being surface to core through me.

At last her body pauses for a frozen, urgent thrust and we all feel her vibrating shudder through the tensile connection I hold. His smile widens at her guttural, primal sounds as she peaks, and he shakes me slightly, with the sure, delicate touch of a master. The slight motion sends subtle movement through me, each slight tremor against her clit helping her ride one ecstatic wave after another.

Finally she lolls back, body slack in my soft lengths. Finally I feel his grip loosen. I am stretched, loose, but still filled with the electric sex that seems to glow from her. He unwinds me slowly from her skin, gently from between her tender lips, still slick with her spent need. Again I stroke her body as he draws me across and through each twist.

Her muscles flex tentatively against unwelcome release. I have left my mark, twining soft red patterns here and there where our connection was strongest, dimpling her skin with the witness of our shared strength and need. She makes a soft sound of regret as I am finally lifted from her shoulders, but I know our separation will be short. He winds me neat and firm before pressing me gently against her heart, and I feel it quicken with surprise and delight. She did not know, as I did, that we were bound the moment I touched between her legs. The realization brings a delighted smile to us both.

I know that long after he is gone she will take me to her bed and draw me tight across her skin again. I wonder if it will be her hand that pulls me, or his, or another's. One thing I know: she and I have lengths of pleasure and knots of connection yet to explore.

They hug, holding me tight between their bodies. I feel their hearts pound against each other through my twists and coils. Connected, we three are one in this exquisite moment, unique, ephemeral, beautiful.

I am the rope that binds.

DISCOVERING HER WRISTS, BOUND

Saskia Walker

C arrie heard the front door click open then shut, and paused, hands deep in the washing-up bowl. She'd been listening out, waiting for Mike to arrive. Before she had a chance to move he strode into the kitchen and pounced, closing in behind her and pressing her hard against the edge of the sink.

"Well hello to you too." She chuckled when he nuzzled her neck and kissed her behind her ear.

"Got you trapped. No escape now." He cupped her breasts from behind.

Trapped with Mike. Bliss. They'd only been living together for two months and were still learning their way. Carrie couldn't have been happier to hear the possessive, lusty tone in his comment. She savored the feel of him, so hard and masculine at her back. While he touched and caressed her she stared down at the gardens below their first-floor apartment and then across to the houses opposite, but it soon became a blur, because he was manhandling her breasts, squeezing them and massaging them through her shirt. Her flesh responded instantly, sensation needling into her nipples and tugging at her very center. She gripped the edge of the sink with her gloved hands.

He liked to do this, to explore her body from behind, but he hadn't done it like this before, not here, not right at the window. Nevertheless, the situation made her hot, and there was something about him, an edge of power that made her feel as if she might waver on her feet if he stepped away.

"Mike, someone might see."

He growled low under his breath and ducked his head to kiss the side of her neck. When he lifted his head she glanced over her shoulder. Was that a twinkle in his eyes?

"So, was it a good day?" He'd had an important meeting, but she didn't want to make a big deal of it.

"Even better now."

She smiled to herself. "You're going to play hard to get, huh?"

That probably indicated the meeting had gone well, but she couldn't be sure.

He ignored her question. Instead he nodded his head at the sink. "I thought we were going out to eat, no matter what? You're not cooking are you?"

"I was just keeping busy."

"Turn around, let me look at you."

Carrie did so, removing her sudsy rubber gloves, tugging them off slowly and casting them aside as she turned.

"The way you do that," he commented, and shook his head, "I've never met a woman who can make taking off household gloves look quite so much like a striptease."

She laughed softly. "So that's why you wanted me."

"One of many reasons."

It never got old, hearing that. His gaze covered her, slowly, approvingly.

She simmered. Reaching for his tie, she undid it and slid it back and forth under his collar as she looked up at him. He made her want to dance, and she moved her hips, holding his gaze while she did so. "What do I have to do to find out what happened in the meeting today, tie you up and torture you?"

The look in his eyes became brooding. He reached for her hands, grasping her around both wrists, as if to still her. There was a distinct set to his mouth, sensual, almost a pout. He was horny.

"If anyone is going to be doing any tying up around here it'll be me," he responded without hesitation. Something in his expression changed.

The way he held her wrists so tightly surprised her.

Why did I say that, about tying him up? It had just come out, spur of the moment.

She glanced down at his strong hands wrapped around her slender wrists. It stimulated something in her, something deeper than desire. A need she had not yet discovered.

"Now why would you want to tie me up?" She was eager to know where this might go.

"Oh, I can think of a dozen good reasons."

Her heartbeat had become erratic. She'd never seen him quite like this before. He was always passionate, often impetuous, but this...this edgy look in his eyes, and the way he held her so tightly. It made her want to know more, like how deeply it ran. "Give me one reason, make it a good one."

"Because I'd like to have you thoroughly under my control, so I could touch you and taste you and have my way with you while you have absolutely no say in the matter." He tempered the comment by giving her a suggestive smile.

She swallowed. "I hadn't realized you were into...that."

Mike laughed softly. "I'm not." There was that wicked glint

in his eye again. He shrugged. "Maybe I am. I certainly like the idea of having you at my mercy."

The teasing, jokey mood had altered because the tension between them heightened by the moment. He still had ahold of her wrists and his expensive silk tie was crushed in her fisted hand. She stared at him, aware that her face had flushed and he'd be able to tell just how aroused she was.

"Want to give it a try?" His voice was so low as he asked the question it was a whisper, a suggestive whisper, and he was so close to her that she felt his breath warm on her face. What would it be like, letting him have his way as he so casually put it? It unnerved her, but it also excited her immensely.

He could tell—the recognition was there in his eyes. She nodded.

He tugged the tie from her hand and looped it around her wrists, tying them together.

Carrie stared down at her wrists, bound.

The significance of it hit her, steeping her in arousal. Her wrists had never been bound together before, but she'd agreed to it and she liked the way it made her feel. It meant she was his, completely.

When she met his gaze, he nodded, then tugged on the loose end of the tie, drawing her along with him as he moved to leave the kitchen.

"Mike," she whispered as she followed, shocked that he was leading her that way and yet breathless with arousal because he was. It felt wrong, like she was a naughty pet that had to be restrained, but it was such a turn-on.

He didn't pause. Instead he led her to the bedroom where he encouraged her to stand by the bed. For some reason she found it hard to meet his gaze.

He faced her. "Lift your chin. Look at me."

It was a command, and it made her breath catch in her throat. Arousal pulled heavily inside her, building heat between her thighs. Tension filled the room, clinging around them like static. She felt his scrutiny, his lust, and it set loose a demanding ache at her core. Lifting her eyelids, she looked at him.

When he took action and undid the buttons on her shirt, Carrie found it hard to breathe. He pulled the shirt open, then eased the cups of her bra down, lifting her breasts up so that they rested on the cups. He had her on display.

"That's better," he commented, then reached for the hem of her tight-fitting skirt. Tugging it up around her hips, he pulled her panties down to her ankles, then encouraged her to step out of them. Once she had, he nodded at the bed.

Moving awkwardly Carrie sat, then lay back. As soon as she did, Mike lifted her wrists and looped the tie though the wooden struts on their headboard. He knotted it there, so that her arms were up over her head and her breasts were lewdly displayed.

Carrie swallowed down her nerves.

Mike moved to the end of the bed and folded his arms across his chest as he looked down at her.

"This is what you wanted," she murmured, suddenly not sure. She felt so exposed with her breasts lolling, her skirt up and her pussy bared that way. More than that, the restraint forced her into a different mood. It made something give way inside her, and she rolled her head on the pillow, her pulse racing.

"It is now."

She shot him a querying look. "Why?"

"You're offering yourself to me."

"I always offer myself to you."

"Yes, but this is different."

Carrie nodded. "It is."

It was a statement of trust, handing the power over to him completely.

Mike knelt one knee on the bed and wrenched her legs apart, spread-eagling her, making her gasp. Before she had a chance to say anything, he put his hand between her legs, and she had to blink back the flash of sheer pleasure that shot through her groin when he stroked his fingers over her clit and down the groove of her pussy.

"I want to make you come."

She whimpered.

"You want that too, don't you?" While he spoke he stared down at her.

His gaze made her splayed pussy feel even more deliciously vulnerable and exposed. "Yes."

He squeezed her clit, locking it between two fingers and rocking his hand.

She half sat, her wrists jolting against the headboard. She sank back, whimpering. As she did, she felt warm liquid run down between her buttocks.

"So wet," he murmured and ducked down between her legs, his mouth closing over her clit.

Her back arched against the bed, the tension in her hips and shoulders intensifying. "Mike, please."

"Okay. I know. Just a little longer. Let me adore you."

Let me adore you. That made her melt. Physically, and emotionally.

He squeezed her clit again, his tongue moving from her entrance up to the tip where he swirled it, making her crazy.

"I need you inside me," she cried out, "please."

Breathing over her sensitive flesh, he sighed.

That made it worse. "Mike...?"

He moved his hands away from her pussy. "Are you begging?"

Carrie shook back her hair, relief hitting her when she saw the bulk of his erection inside his pants. "Yes, Mike, I'm begging you. Please, please fuck me."

He stood up, a smile passing over his face, and went for his belt.

She watched as he undid his clothing and let each item fall to the floor. When his cock bounced free, slapping against his belly as he cast aside the last of his clothing, her sex clutched, longing to be filled by that glorious erection.

But he made her wait. Starting at her toes he kissed the length of her legs. As he closed in on her pussy she raised her hips, ready to receive him inside. But Mike shifted his attention and kissed her breasts, her breastbone, and then he pushed her skirt higher still so he could kiss her abdomen, right above her pussy where she ached for release.

Carrie writhed, her wrists automatically tugging against her tethers, her hands eager to caress him and encourage him closer. The fact that she couldn't do that made her wilder still, more needy than she ever had been. And her clothing, barely undone and tangled, only added to the problem. It hampered her movement and emphasized her inability to control herself or her situation.

By the time he climbed over her and moved into position, her entire body had misted with damp heat and her breathing had become shallow and fast.

"This really suits you," he commented.

In one knowing thrust he filled her.

The room spun, her eyes clamped shut and she heard her own wild cry as she came, suddenly, and spectacularly.

"Oh, yeah, that feels good, just like I knew it would." Even as she moaned aloud in her climax and her core spasmed, he rode in and out, speeding all the while, taking her deeper still.

Mike urged her on, taking shallower thrusts as he readied to come, his body rubbing against her tender clit. She was lost to it, her sex clenching and unclenching, and as it did it set off another rolling wave of pleasure. She moaned, begged for mercy.

Still he pushed her on, his face against hers, his breath hot on her cheek. "I'm coming."

One last thrust, deep and hard, and she focused long enough to hold him tight while his cock jerked and he doused her in his hot semen.

When he rolled free it took several minutes for her to muster the question she wanted to ask. "Was this you celebrating something?"

"Yes." That was all he said at first. Eventually he lifted onto his elbow at her side and smiled down at her. "The meeting went well; I got the promotion."

Pride blossomed in her chest. "That's fabulous news. So... you wanted to celebrate by taking charge of me, huh?"

"Uh-huh," he said as he ran his hands over her defenseless breasts, seemingly taking even more pleasure in the act than usual, because she couldn't stop him.

"Are you going to want to celebrate this way every time you get good news?"

He ran his fingers over her bound wrists and she thought he was going to undo her. "No," he responded.

That leveled her elation somewhat.

"More often than that," he added, taking his hand away, leaving her tied.

She laughed, pleased. "You really did want to tie me up."

"Yes, but you suggested it."

"I did not!"

"Yes you did, you asked if you would have to tie me up to find out what happened at the meeting. You can't expect to say something like that to a man and not have him ready to pounce. Like a red flag to a bull, my dear. So where did that come from, my little spitfire?"

"I have no idea."

"So you accept full responsibility?"

"No!" Again she laughed. "It was your fault. You said you'd got me trapped at the sink. That must have triggered my comment."

"Oh, I see, my fault." His smile lingered.

When he began to move his hips again, and Carrie felt his erection growing, she lifted her brows and nodded up at her bound wrists. "I thought we were going out to eat, no matter what?"

"I'll have something delivered, and I'll feed you myself. You're far too busy to go out."

"Busy?"

"Yeah, you're all tied up."

"And you're going to keep me this way?"

"For the time being, yes. Any objections?"

Carrie sighed with pleasure. "None at all."

IN HER SIGHTS

Kiki DeLovely

I once watched an artist painting a portrait of his lover. Witnessed the lascivious nature of his brush dipping into the pigment, the amative blending of colors just so on the palette, before he ever touched tip to canvas. Working assiduously to infuse his lover's very soul into the eyes; languidly lingering on the lips, introducing sex to the mouth. He studied his subject's face so intently, so intimately, his lover shackled under the weight of his regard.

I've seen that artist's look in Lux's eyes, *una mirada muy particular,* sensed that fixed stare effusive and sumptuous against my surface, and then felt her go deeper. Entering my fleshy sex with her fist, farther still with her gaze.

My clit skips a beat.

I can't get past the way she's caught me and holds me captive with that gaze—knowing and profoundly intense. She twists her wrist one last time and my cunt clamps down as I submit to the waves rippling, then ripping, through me. "Mmmmmmm…

that's my good girl." And then she's gone. Pulls out of me with not the slightest warning and I cry out, suck in and am left wanting. So painfully wanting. My shyness begging to break away and cast my eyes downward, to bring my hand to my face and deflect at least a small portion of it all. *Me muero de la timidez*—I might just be the first case known to womankind who succumbs to shyness. But just as this thought flashes hot across my flesh, her control seeps into my abyss and I'm hooked. Inescapably. Tethered up in her resolve.

This type of unrelenting attention would have once put me on edge. And not the sort of edge I usually enjoy. The past couple of decades (and the multitude of lovers therein) have reworked my self-view and these days *mi panza* gets as much love as my curvaceous hips—those that act as grand parentheses for such a gorgeously rounded belly. And if a hot butch wants more than—*much* more than—a handful of *tetas tan grandes como las mías,* she also gets the thighs that make the most amazing *swooshing* sound as they rub together when I make my way through a crowded shopping mall or dance into the deep blue of the night.

The intent behind that gaze of hers weighs heavily, and she knows it. I am all woman, *una mujer de cierta edad,* no less; and yet she can make me feel so young, the way I experience myself reflected in her *sensualidad.* She could certainly see it written all over me—ink rising from my pores and pooling into script, skirting its way across my skin, telling a story of the girl drowning in her eyes—it's an easy read, altogether too lucid. Lux chooses this moment to remove her glasses and take a step back without a moment's hesitation nor a second's glance away.

I suppress my timidity and study her figure just as she's poring over mine. Both of us just a hair shy of six feet, of Amazonian build, though I would definitely qualify as more of a glamazon. I'm all things girly—painted eyelashes and petticoats—a softness in stark contrast to Lux's solid, athletic physique. She's the type of warrior who wouldn't hesitate to remove her right breast should it interfere with her weapon of choice. Still she takes great pride and pleasure in her body. As do I. Such great, overpowering pleasure she inflicts upon me. She need not remove a thing in order to command the sharp piece of steel in her hand.

I find it impossible to be in her presence without brimming *con amor propio*—this love of mine elevates my pride to new levels. I feel as though the earth is moving too swiftly; I've tripped and stumbled into the sea—the adrenaline coursing through my veins from the fearful lust is only a small part of the swaying sensation. Lux has a dizzying effect on my sense of balance and reality; I feel myself slipping away.

She's shaking her head back and forth. Slowly. Ever so slowly. Staring into me with eyes that say, *Fuck, yes* to every last turn my body takes, *todas las curvas de mi cuerpo*. Something about it—an action that traditionally reads as *no* when she really means just the opposite—consumes me with desire. She devours me with that look. Captivating in every sense of the word—I am her captive. After our first several days spent together, I felt like watching her do that was so imprinted on my clit that I could come just from having her shake her head at me from across the room. And at the very least, it made my knees give out. It always does.

Lucky for me, she likes me on them.

Lux is detail orientated, as am I; her focus makes it abundantly clear that none of my efforts while down there are lost on her. She relishes the sensuousness of the senses—the wet, lustrous noises of the head of her cock hitting the back of my throat; the sight of me thrusting enthusiastically against the shaft, crimson red lips wrapped around the length of her; the pressure of me fucking her back while she fucks my face; the essence of my ravenous cunt wafting up. She opens her mouth to breathe in every last note, tasting metallic.

The arc of her cock is just a continuation of that of her thighs. Its bulge against the fly of her jeans whenever she packs—the perfect complement to the cleavage continually spilling out of my lacy-edged, demi-cup bra. When her quads flex under my palms, all that magnificent energy billows up, pulsing through her cock, and into me. Her stare still as heavy and restrictive as ever, my tongue bound under the invasion of her instrument. Lux swells and shudders; I work harder and faster. Sucking her off, making her moan, "Oooooh, yes... That's it, *garotinha*, take it all." (Lux just loves to throw her bits of Portuguese around, as she does her weight—fully knowing both can pin me in an instant. She may not be fluent, but hell, my Spanish could use some cleaning up and my cunt certainly doesn't seem to discriminate.)

"So. Fucking. Good." She punctuates each word with a thrust, testing just how much abuse my vocal cords can take.

What gets her off more than how I deliciously pique her senses is her ability to pierce me with that gaze. Lecherously peering, Lux pries into the depths of me, the heart of me, her dick growing harder at the discovery of something so depraved and pure. Her orgasm mounting hastily at my naive nescience in letting her in. As she pierces me farther, the metallic flavor wraps around her tongue and spills down her throat, filling her up.

I want so badly to watch her watching me, to see the story her eyes tell of how pleased she is with everything happening below, to witness how she possesses me so thoroughly with just a look. But I can't. My eyelids refuse to open when I'm choking so on *su verga tan larga* that I can hardly suck in any air while

I suck her down. I suppose it's a question of bodily physics and mine adhere to the shut-eyed-cock-choking phenomenon. I pull her out just momentarily to steal a peek and witness the glorious look of dominating satisfaction carved into Lux's face.

"Well done, baby girl." Warmth and pride on her breath. "Now get up." I long to dig my nails deeper into her luscious cheeks, clutch at the meat of that divine ass while I'm swallowing her whole; but knowing better than to argue with that tone, I rise. Markedly laconic, her words are sparse at times like these but always poignant. Pointed. As sharp as her stare and steel. "Facedown on the bed," she instructs. Later the words will pour off of her tongue and spill all over me. Flood my mind and my senses. This moment exists almost entirely in the unspoken desire that blazes from her eyes; she descends farther, filling me with more than I thought possible. I'm voluntarily enslaved.

Words cannot circumnavigate these waters.

I hear the sound of her spit hitting her palm and I swear I can almost feel her ease it down the length of her *polla tan magnífica;* oh, how I adore that dick of hers. Then she's brusquely grabbing me by my love handles—I knew there was a reason for such an aptly named part of the female body—and pounding *mi chocha* into next week. Just as I begin to think that a fuck couldn't get more exquisite, Lux shifts her angle ever so slightly, and an entirely new sensation washes over me. My pussy is gushing with the feel of her violent tempest gaining speed, threatening to tear me apart. I sneak a glance over my shoulder, delighting in the sweat gathering across the arch of her bicep, over the top lip of her upturned snarl. She frees up one hand, keeping the other firmly gripped around the flesh of my right hip, and rakes her fingers through my hair while she rams me from behind. Making a fist around the strands just above the nape of my neck, she pulls my head back with just enough force to hear me whimper, then pushes against me, getting even better leverage. My face takes on the creases of the pillow.

She won't let me come. Not yet. *La tortura.* She revels in it. So she pulls out. Leaving me wanting yet again, despite my protests. "No, no, no, no...*por fas, cariño...*" Not acknowledging a single word I've uttered, though I know she understands me perfectly. Sometimes she likes to back off of me even farther when I beg like that. Unfortunately, now is one of those times. All part of the game we play.

She regards me with such intensity I feel desperately vulnerable and still somehow safe enough to let her in. Though she needs no invitation. Lux fully knows this is hers for the taking. So she takes it and I accept my role as a willing sacrifice, laying my body down before her. I allow her to forge away at her own pace; accept whatever is left when she is done. Her eyes taste every last curve.

She takes her time and drags the stainless steel slowly across my skin, trailing where her gaze left off, the tip occasionally digging into the plumpness of my thighs, my ass, testing their give. And, *oh*, do I give. The cold, keen edge gives rise to a chill blushing across my surface and I feel her lust tear into me, shredding any last lingering defenses. I only wish her blade could penetrate me so deeply. Before I can finish wishing and just as I gasp loudly enough for the neighbors to hear, my remaining lingerie hits the floor in pieces and I wonder if I didn't perhaps wish too hard. Lux's knife is too sharp for this kind of play, too near to breaking flesh. And if I don't take control of my involuntary shaking, she will.

She retracts her blade and flips me deftly. I sink into her pervasive gaze. Instinctively she holds court in two opposing spaces—easily reigning over me as the outsider peering in while simultaneously occupying an expanse within, cutting to the core of me. Lux has set her sights on me *y no me suelta*. There'll be no letting up until she's taken all she needs and I'm left barely breathing. I inhale one last time as she crashes over me, crashing into me with those eyes. Those eyes that see me, that search me out. Those eyes that take me under.

DEEPER

Beatrix Ellroy

Grace crossed her legs and glared at the other people in the café. The table was currently empty save her gear, but it wouldn't be for long if the crowd got any bigger. She churned through her work as face after face mercifully turned away from her. As she finalized the urgent bit of code that had hauled her from home in search of a decent cup of coffee, one of the men in the masses caught her eye. He walked over, coffee in hand, and she studied him as he came closer. She'd seen him at the café before, admired his body, but had never been able to work out why he was familiar; she couldn't remember his name, or even why she might have known him. Not until he spoke.

"Do you mind if I sit here?"

His voice was dark; sweet bourbon with a hint of gravel and it took her right back to her awkward teen years, spent in tiny, illicit clubs listening to an ever-changing list of little bands trying to make their mark on an indifferent crowd. He'd made his mark, cut a few albums, then dropped off the radar. She'd followed his career the whole way through, even as an adult who really should have known better. He'd starred in her fantasies for far longer than was strictly appropriate.

He was different now, that was true, but still magnetic. Still handsome, but his arms were bulkier, shoulders broader. His entire body had filled out (her mind whispered *matured*) and he looked like he could do anything he put his mind to. His hair was shorn close to the scalp, but still thick, and dark but for the streaks of gray and silver at the edges. His eyes were as intense as they'd ever been. He was still hawk nosed, still full lipped. Her mind raced with those old desires, awoken by his closeness. She looked him in the eye and smiled.

"Not at all. Miko isn't it? I used to watch you play."

His eyes widened slightly. "Really? I wouldn't have taken you for being nearly old enough to have seen me at a club." His smile was automatic, insincere, with his eyes already drifting to watch the stream of people outside the window.

"Flattery, particularly the empty type, will get you nowhere." She sipped her coffee, waiting. The silence stretched, almost awkward, but Grace was no stranger to waiting. He turned to her, as if startled by her response. He let his eyes roam and after a long moment, he smiled.

"Oh, I'm sorry. It's somewhat of an ingrained response to meeting such a pretty lady. Doesn't change the intent. Shall we start again?"

He reached one broad hand over the table. "I'm Miko, as you're apparently aware. My thanks for sharing your table, but I don't believe you've given me your name?" His smile was tilted, but genuine. Grace reached out in response; his hand engulfed hers, calloused against the softness of her skin.

"Grace. I'm just finishing up actually."

He held her hand for a beat too long, then lingeringly let it go. Her stomach fluttered at the contact and she almost wanted to squirm; she had lusted after Miko incredibly badly for years and here he was. She had never imagined he smelled so good. Coffee and vanilla, sweet and bitter with hidden depths.

"Stay awhile, if you can. I gather compliments on your looks aren't going to keep you interested though. No matter how lyrical I wax about the curve of your leg, or the depth of color in your eyes?" He seemed amused, the skin around his eyes creasing as he smiled and shifted his chair closer to hers. "Should I compliment your choice of tech then? Coffee? Or maybe your taste in music?"

"It's been a while since I listened to your band, Miko. A good long while." Grace began breathing just a touch too rapidly. His proximity was simply too much. His hand, curved around the mug, led to a muscled and hairy forearm, flexing as he swirled his coffee. A sudden image flashed through her mind, and she almost blushed. Almost. She hadn't learned self-control for nothing though. "I did notice you released your entire back catalogue online last year. Nice move that was. A bit of increased revenue in the non-digital goods and no skin off your back since your albums were out of stock anyway." She smiled then, thinking of the first album she'd ever bought, close to ten years ago now. It was one of his and she was sure it was still tucked away somewhere. The pictures on the liner, his body crossed with leather and strapped down and bound, had fueled her fantasies for years.

Miko shrugged. "It made sense at the time. I'm busy with other business avenues now, so releasing the back catalogue did nothing but introduce us to a whole new fan base." He raised an eyebrow. "Nice of you to keep track though. Just how big of a fan are you anyway?" This time, Grace did blush, her cheeks burning. His laughter was loud, and honest. She laughed too, caught out by her own desires.

Desires that didn't seem quite so unobtainable anymore.

"Oh I'm a big fan, no doubt about that. You starred in many a daydream when I was young." His eyebrows shot up at that.

"Did I now? Let me try and guess since I've heard enough of these. Did you save me from my hellish ways and marry me, or did you follow me into debauchery?" He paused. "If it was the latter, please feel free to elaborate." His grin was wicked.

Grace sipped her coffee too, trying to slow her breathing. "A little from column A, a little from column B. The best ones had a bit of both." She smiled and startled a laugh from Miko.

"Really? Please tell. The reality was not nearly so fun, I have to say." His tone was light but his eyes held hers. Dark, almost black in the dim light of the café. She felt adrenaline singing along her spine, her skin tingling, joyous abandon rising up as if to carry her onward.

She took a breath and plunged.

"The old fantasies aren't nearly as interesting as the new ones. The old ones were all variations on a theme—I was inexperienced, malleable, so they were all about you teaching me. Dominating me." Her voice was low, and dark. He leaned forward, unconsciously, shifting to the edge of his seat to face her. She shifted too, then reached a hand across, slowly, and curved her fingers around his neck with her thumb resting lightly on his throat. "Nowadays I know what I want." She leaned in closer, pressed her thumb down and felt his breath in her hair then murmured. "I want to take you home, I want you naked in my bed and I want to fuck you." Grace eased back into her seat. "Your choice of course. We could sit here and finish our coffees if you like. Talk music and revenue streams, then say good-bye." She took a sip of her coffee. "It'd be a fascinating conversation I'm sure. Not as fascinating as what I'll do to you when you're on your knees though."

He leaned back and pushed his coffee to the side. He looked at her, obviously weighing up the offer. She smiled back, open and daring, radiating that self-control she'd developed over the years, that confidence that seemed to draw a certain kind of man to her. And to his knees for her.

"Let's go then." His voice was dark, and fierce with promise.

The short walk back to Grace's apartment thrummed with tension; they barely touched but were never more than a breath away from each other. She could feel desire pooling in her bones, making her swell and slicken. They barely got into the elevator before she pushed him against the wall and kissed him. Hard and vicious, she tasted and bit and sucked at his lips. Her hands framed his face as her body pressed his against the wall, his hands grasping her hips. The doors opened and they broke apart; Grace turned and strode down the hall, leading him to her apartment. She got the door closed before giving in to the temptation and kissing him again. She bit her way down his neck and left a trail of reddened flesh in her wake.

"You know, I almost wish for your long hair back. I would have loved to drag you by your hair to my bed and then pin you down with it while I fucked you in the ass."

Miko moaned. Loud and desperate.

"Yes, fuck, yes." His voice was rough and his hands were still pressing into her hips, pinpoints of bruising pain. She ran her nails down the length of his arms, and then brought the palm of his hand to her face.

"I want to fuck you, Miko; I want you naked and splayed and open." Grace murmured into his palm then bit, not gently, at his wrist. "Are you okay with that?"

Miko pulled her firmly against his body, his cock hard and huge behind the denim of his jeans. "Yes, I am so okay with that. Christ, I want you inside me."

She felt herself quiver and contract as he spoke. She led him through to her bedroom, gripping his wrist. Her bed was low, the sheets black and the light coming through the window was bright. She pushed him toward the bed and began to unbutton her shirt. "Take your clothes off. All of them." She was gratified to see him obey, pulling his shirt over his head, revealing the lines and patterns of muscles and ink-stained skin; a small tattoo ran over one shoulder blade, a line of hieroglyphs contained in a cartouche. She watched him slip his shoes and socks off, then unbuckle his belt.

His jeans dropped and she took a deep breath. This was really happening. Miko was here. In her bedroom.

She pulled her shirt and her skirt off and kicked them under the bed, along with her shoes and her stockings. Miko turned to her, still in his underwear, and glanced uncertainly at the window. Grace laughed then pressed a button and a decorated screen lowered, dulling the light slightly, throwing shadows across the room. Only then did he slip his thumbs into the waistband of his underwear and slide them down his thighs.

Grace felt dizzy for a moment, caught between two desires. She wanted him, fucked and splayed open and hers. She also wanted him inside her, driving into her. His cock was heavy, thick and long and hard already.

She sat on the bed, still in her knickers and bra, and beckoned him closer, pulling him to stand between her legs. His cock stood firm as she ran her hands up his legs, dragging her nails over the skin of his thighs. She brushed her hand over his balls, pushing his cock to one side, and nuzzled the skin over his hip, dragging her teeth over the bony jut of it. She paused and reached beneath the bed to pull out a small case and place it on the chest beside them. She flicked open the latch and drew out a small tea box filled with condoms, then leaned forward and

licked Miko's cock from base to tip, tracing a circle over the end
before she rolled a condom down his length.

She stood up then and kissed him again. The smell of his
skin was intense at such a short distance and she ran her tongue
along his jawline, tasting his stubble and sweat. She could feel his
breathing increase, his heart rapidly beating. "Now, Miko, just
how badly do you want me to fuck you?" She felt his breathing
hitch, and tasted the sweat on his brow.

"Fuck." His voice was strained. "Fuck me. Now, however
you want, just fuck me." Grace could feel a slight tremble in
his arms. She laughed and kissed him again, tasting the bitter
coffee.

"Eager aren't you? Can't wait to feel me filling you, driving
into you, can you?"

She walked around him and opened the drawers set against
one wall. Nestled against crisp white cotton, an array of differently sized and shaped dildos rested. "Come here and choose.
Whichever you want, or think you can handle." As he looked
over the selection his hands danced against the wood of the
drawer and he bit slightly at his bottom lip. She wanted desperately to fuck his face every time his tongue darted out to soothe
the bitten places. He placed his hand, hesitantly, on one of her
largest, a purple-tinted monstrosity. Her quim tingled, remembering how full and fucked she felt with that inside her. She
smiled and drew it out. She also grabbed one of the midsized
dildos, black and menacing, but smaller. She had no intention
of making this uncomfortable, but if he wanted the intensity,
she could provide it.

"Go lie on the bed, Miko, I'll be there in a moment." She ran
a hand down his side as she said it, the pushed him toward the
bed. She needed an orgasm before she started, or it would all go
too quickly. Grace wanted this to last. She pulled off her under-

wear and pulled on a harness, one providing easy access to her already slick cunt and clit. Miko lay on the bed, his cock hard and heavy. Grace stepped onto the bed, feeling it sway beneath her feet, and stood over his prone body.

"Would you like to be restrained? I've got a nice selection of cuffs and ties and ropes around." She dropped to kneel over his chest, her slickness pressed into his chest and the purple, silicon cock resting near his face. "Or I could hold you down. Maybe just order you to stay still." Miko was breathing fast. "Are you good at following orders? Or do you need some encouragement?" She gently tweaked one nipple. "What do you need, Miko?"

Miko closed his eyes and breathed. "Tie me down. I'll say stop if I need you to let me up. I am...terrible at following orders." Grace smiled and Miko's eyes opened, staring into hers. Then she swung herself up and off him to gather up her ropes and ties. She hung one rope from the ceiling, hooks and clips already in place. She tied Miko's hands together above his head and then clipped the rope into a hook embedded in the headboard.

"Now you're nice and restrained, I'm going to fuck your face until I come." She knelt over him once more, and kissed him before moving forward to grind her clit against his tongue. She put one hand against his forehead and balanced herself with the other, moving her hips. His tongue was magnificent, pressing against her already swollen clit. He moved to dart his tongue inside her and she moaned, loud and sudden. "Fuck yes, Miko, do that again."

As he licked and sucked and fucked her with his tongue, Grace moved both hands to the headboard and stilled her hips; Miko needed no assistance with his ministrations. She could feel the orgasm building, his tongue playing along her clit and fucking deep inside her. She began to gasp and moan as the orgasm rolled, her body trembling as it hit, hard and fast. It subsided as fast as it had arrived and she moved off Miko's face now glistening with her wetness. She leaned down to kiss him, tasting herself overlying the bitter coffee and the scent of him. He kissed her back, needy and wanting.

Grace drew away and knelt at the bottom of the bed watching him squirm. She ran her fingers along the arches of his feet and the bones of his ankle. "Miko, I'm going to clip you to the ceiling. It can take your weight, so I can position you however I like. Right now, for this, I want you on your knees close to the edge here, back to me, leaning over."

Miko strained upward, knees splayed and cock leaking, and answered, "Yes, Grace."

Grace unclipped his hands and pulled him upward, clipping his hands high above his head and tying off the rope to another hook. She rather liked the look, his arms long and lean and his shoulders straining just slightly.

"I think I might leave you like that for a bit. Just while I start preparing to fuck you." She walked in front of him and drew lube and a small box of nitrile gloves from the bedside table. "You aren't allergic to lube are you?"

When Miko shook his head she spread some over her gloved hands and the purple monstrosity at her groin, still luridly colored beneath the condom. He watched as her hands spread the lube, and she could see his cock twitch. Once the lube was spread she lowered his hands; they were still over his head but he leaned forward now, balancing with his arse jutting out and his legs spread. She walked behind him and ran one finger over his perineum.

"Now, remember to say stop if it isn't working for you."

She slid one finger into his arsehole. He took it easily and she added a second, then a third, realizing the purple cock might not be too big after all. She felt herself clench again, thinking about

just how willing he was. She drove her fingers into his arsehole, twisting them and brushing against his prostate almost
randomly. Miko moaned and gasped each time she did and it
was a struggle not to continue doing it, just for the sounds he
made. Eventually she added a fourth finger and Miko moaned
long and hard, gasping her name like a prayer.

"Fuck, Grace, fuck me."

She withdrew her fingers and Miko pushed backward,
keening at the loss of sensation; in response she steadied his
hips and slapped his arse, once. He stilled, breathing heavily,
pushing his face into his arm. "Oh god, Grace, please fuck me,
I can't take it anymore. Please."

She brushed more lube over Miko's arsehole and the purple
dildo, and then pushed the head of it inside him. Even after her
finger-fucking, even after four fingers pushing into him, there
was still resistance. She waited for him to adjust, reading the
strain in his shoulders as discomfort more than pleasure or even
pain. She swept one lubed hand from the base of his cock to the
tip and he moaned once more, pushing back and taking more of
the purple cock in.

Grace asked, "How are you doing? This is a monster of a
thing to take—worth it, but big."

Miko was silent for a while, panting slightly. "Fuck, I want it,
I want you to fuck me with it, I *need* it, but Christ it's huge."

Grace kneaded her thumbs into the base of his spine. "It's
okay, Miko, we can take as long as you want. You don't have
to take it all now." She realized that she definitely wanted him
to take it all, but she also wanted to do this again and again. It
would be worth building up to this, working up to it until he
begged her for it. She swept her hand over his still hard cock and
again he pushed back and grunted and swayed, head down and
shoulders tense.

"I want to see you take this all, I want to fuck you hard with it, but right now, I just want to fuck you." Grace pulled out, slowly and gently. Miko's arsehole gaped and she pushed four fingers back inside and he whimpered again as she slowly thrust them back and forth, scissoring them and stretching him. With her other hand she replaced the purple dildo with the black one she picked up from beside the bed; it had the advantage of being slightly smaller and possessing a small protrusion perfectly formed to nestle against her clit. She slid a condom on, lubed it up and positioned herself to fuck him again.

"Brace yourself Miko."

She pulled her fingers from him, grasped his cock and slid the dildo home, one long thrust until her hips pressed against his arse. He cried out, loud and shocked and needy, and she did the same, feeling his cock jump in her hand and the small nub from the dildo press against her clit in imitation of her thrust.

"You're so fucking open now, with only a little try of my purple cock." Grace's voice was strained with desire. "So fucking open and wide, taking this one in to the hilt. I could probably fist you; slide my whole hand inside you." Miko moaned and pushed against her, shifting the pressure on her clit. She withdrew and drove in again.

"Fuck yes, Miko." She took her hand off his cock and he moaned. Grace straightened, then pulled his arsecheeks open wide, and began to slide the dildo back and forth, watching it sink into Miko's arse as she rolled her hips back and forth, relishing the gape and press of his stretched arse and the slide and pressure against her clit. He gasped as she fucked him harder, still slowly, but each thrust driving him forward. He hung from the ceiling, legs spread and arms pulled tight above his head. She wanted to make it last, take her time, but desire was like electricity beneath her skin.

She reached around and grabbed his cock once more and placed one hand over his shoulder to hold him in place as she fucked him faster. She brushed her thumb over the head of his cock, then her hand over his balls. She felt them tighten and took her hand away to grip his shoulders hard with both, slamming into his arse, angling against his prostate, pushing the nub of the dildo hard against her clit, driving her over the edge. She thrust hard through her own orgasm, feeling his shoulders tense and strain as she pushed him up and over the edge in turn. Miko moaned and swore as he came, fierce and fast. She kept the dildo pressed into him, against him, as he trembled through his orgasm.

As he recovered she slid the dildo gently from his arsehole and drew the come-filled condom from his twitching cock, then let the ropes down from the ceiling. He lay down while she undid the harness and let it drop to the floor. Her own desire was banked, still simmering and shivering beneath her skin, but Miko was loose-limbed and soft from the exertion, lying facedown on the bed. She traced over the hieroglyphs on his shoulders, pressing into the quivering muscles as she waited for him to come down. After a few moments he spoke.

"You are a fucking terror, Grace." He rolled over to face her. "I thought you were going to fuck me with the purple thing and I couldn't work out if I should be screaming stop or not, and then you were in there to the hilt and I swear I saw God." His chest was still heaving and his breathing labored. "I haven't been fucked like that in a long time. Christ." He reached out and ran his hands over her skin, pressing against her. "I would like to do this again."

Grace smiled. "Of course. I still haven't seen you take the purple cock." She could feel his breath hitch as he settled into the curve of her shoulder, resting a hand on her belly.

"And I haven't fucked you, with or without the purple cock," Miko replied, as his fingers brushed through her damp, intimate curls.

She moaned and spread her legs.

UNWINDING
ALICE

Benjamin Eliot

She's prettiest when I come to get her. Her big brown eyes go wide. It's a very B-horror-movie-babe moment. That deer-in–the-headlights gaze gets me every time. She's always in the walk-in closet. I put her there on a little mountain of throw pillows and blankets. She's trussed up tight with harsh rope. Old-fashioned rope—not the nylon kind. That stuff slips, in my humble opinion.

I come in, already unbuckling my belt. "You've been a good girl," I tell her.

Her eyes are flashing. Her mouth pulled back at the edges by the gag. She looks, to the casual observer, quite terrified. But when I part her legs, she's drenched and she arches her hips up, begging me with her body. She moans and that look in her eyes turns quickly to pleading.

"I'm taking the gag off, but don't talk."

She'll be fraught at this point. Wanting me to fuck her. The bound, gagged and dumped routine is her pleasure. Mine is where she's marked by rope. So she'll have to wait.

She's wriggling at my feet like a fish just pulled onto a boat deck. "Stop wiggling, Alice."

At my tone and the sight of my unbuckled belt and my semi-hard cock beneath my zipper, she freezes. But her gaze is still pleading with me to fuck her. I shake my head because you can't change someone's gaze.

I peel the gag back slowly, shushing and tsking at her to keep her calm.

"Did you enjoy your time in here?"

It has been three hours. Three hours bound and gagged and in the dark of our closet. I cannot imagine someone doing that to me, but I know what it does to my wife. It turns her on, makes her hot, makes her want to fuck. She told me once it was what she desired in lieu of meditation to clear her mind and sharpen her self-awareness. Me...I'd go insane, but this is not about me.

It's about Alice.

Alice remembers and heeds my warning, because she does not speak. She nods in answer to my question. When she moves, one small coil of rope slips and I can see the strawberry imprint of it on her skin. My cock throbs and I take my finger and gently nudge that bit of rope back into place. Not yet.

"Were you too uncomfortable?" I ask. Before she can respond in any fashion, I push my thumb to her lower lip and she sucks it in. Dragging her wet tongue across the pad, wrapping her lips around the tip before drawing it into her sweet mouth with an eager suck.

It all happens in slow motion, and I watch every second of it eagerly. My cock aches and she writhes again on her bed of pillows as if she can sense it. She probably can. She's been immobile in the dark for hours. Alice once told me it often made her feel more than human after she'd been that way for a while.

I force my thumb a bit deeper, and she moans again. I'm tempted to say fuck it. To unwind the rope from her subtly tanned skin, lay her flat, hike her thighs up and apart and just bury myself in her slick cunt. Instead, I take a deep breath and repeat my unanswered question.

"Were you too uncomfortable? Please use words now, Alice."

She pulls her plump lips from my thumb and virtually gasps, "No."

I push my hand between her thighs again, and she slicks my skin with her wetness. I push a finger deep inside her and thrust once, hard, so she wriggles again.

"Are you ready for me?"

She nods. Catches herself. "Yes, Gabe."

I add another finger to the silken tunnel of her cunt and she gasps, arches; her plump mouth, bare of lipstick, works at the air. Again she reminds me of some lovely fish hauled to the deck. Maybe a mermaid if they actually existed.

"Mermaid," I murmur, and her eyes open, flashing at me.

"What?"

"Nothing." I find her clit with my thumb, applying pressure and motion there. She moves up to try to get my fingers deeper and just when I have her right on the edge of orgasm—I can tell because she always starts to chew her lower lip when she's about to come—I pull my fingers out of her.

I paint her lips gently with her own juices. Watch her struggle not to lick her lips and try to persuade me to fuck her now. I want to fuck her now. But I won't.

I put the gag back on. Somehow that always surprises her. I do it almost every time, and yet every time she makes a desperate sound when I push the wet bandana back between her lips. "Just for a minute," I whisper.

Rolled on her belly, she's even more gorgeous. Legs bound in coils and coils of rope. A crosscross of the rough stuff creates an X across her torso. The bottom of the X pulls her nether lips apart just enough that they don't obscure her clitoris. Her wrists are bound behind her back and I know there must be an amazing amount of painful tension there between her jutting shoulder blades. I find the end of the rope binding her legs and begin to unwind her.

My cock strains against my jeans as I uncover the first intricate spirals of rosy indentations on her flesh. I pause when I've got her unraveled up to her knees and flip her up to face me again. I pause and lick the marks the ropes have left on her. Shucking my jeans, I straddle her legs and rub my cock against the rope-branded flesh.

She moans again and that sound seems to spear right through me from the crown of my head to the ache in my balls. I toss my jeans aside and sit back, unwinding her a little more, from her knees to her hips. I'd given her slack from the knees up so I could part her legs and touch her as I had. When her thighs are unbound, they open for me. The most beautiful automatic response I've ever seen.

I slide my cock along the spirals of pink on her skin. I feel the different texture from the marks left by the tight rope with my cock. When she's gasping against the red bandana, I put my mouth to her pussy and lick.

"You were very brave," I tell her. I nuzzle her distended clitoris, stroke it with my tongue. I suck and lave and lap at her until she's crying in earnest. Then I pull back and begin to undo the X that crosses her torso, separating her small, perfect breasts.

I can't help but pet the marks left on her skin. I can't deny my urge to drag my fingertips along the shallow, pale red furrows on her lovely flesh. She gasps as I do it. Her sounds still muffled by the gag. Her body arches up as I stroke her. My touch on those marks, she once told me, is a perfect mix of pain and pleasure. In the moment, she cannot tell if it feels good or hurts.

I bend to drag my tongue over the X of red and capture her nipple as an afterthought. Sucking hard, drawing on her aggressively, the way she likes. It makes her tremble. I move to her other breast, drag my teeth along the pale slope until I grab that nipple with my teeth and tug the rosy red tip. Then I suck and thrust a finger deep inside her cunt.

Behind the gag she cries out. She's trapped in torturous pleasure and it's perfection to watch.

I flip her back to her belly lest I give in and just slide inside her and fuck her. I find the tail end of the rope on her arms and start to unwind. I watch, fascinated and aroused, as Alice slowly grinds her now bare, but still marked hips against the floor. Her toes curl with her effort to get off. When I can't stand watching it anymore, when it has my blood up a bit too high, I smack her once on the ass and say, "Be still, Alice."

I'm unwinding her slowly. Revealing an inch of marked-up skin at a time. Watching her struggle just a bit at the tightness in her shoulders and her back. Listening to her gasp when I pause to chafe the skin that's been trussed up for hours. Left here in the darkness like some captivating, magical night-blooming flower.

"Almost there."

I get to the rope high up on her shoulders and know that if I put my fingers or my cock inside her now she'd be sinfully slick, welcoming.

"Almost there," I mutter again, as much for myself as for her. I've been sitting downstairs for hours laboring over work spreadsheets, but fantasizing about my Alice, tied up in the closet. Gagged. Getting slicker by the moment. Occasionally, I'd make noise so she could hear that I was there. She told me once it's her only real fear. That I'd leave the house while she was in the closet. That something would happen. That I wouldn't come back. I want her worked up, aroused, nearly feral...but not scared like that. Never like that.

"I'd never leave you," I tell her, putting my internal thoughts out for her to hear.

Behind the gag she sighs.

She's utterly bare now but for the lines on her flesh. The pale-red streaks that cross her skin like fading tattoos are lovely. I kiss every inch of her, drag my tongue along the paths left by my hemp. When I reach her pussy, I press her thighs to the ground and hold her there. I put my mouth to her nether lips, snake my tongue between, attack her clitoris with eager laps and licks and nibbles.

She arches up and bucks and makes that frantic noise that always makes my cock just a bit harder no matter how hard it is already.

"You can come, Alice. You've earned it," I say and I press my fingertips to the shallow trenches from the rope on her thighs. I thrust my tongue inside her and then suck her clit again.

Alice comes.

All her pretty ropes are coiled up in the corner. It's like the nest of some mythical bird in here. Pillows and blankets and now coils of rope. I untie the gag and add it to her pile of treasures.

"Gabe, Gabe...Gabriel," she sighs. When she says my full name I know she's fully gone. Lost in the pleasure. Lost in her own little sex scenario. The scene that works her up, does it for her, gets her off.

"I rescued you," I chuckle.

She shuts her eyes, smiling, nodding. She parts her thighs even more and her knees rest upon teal-colored throw pillows. I angle her hips and study the road map of red left by my bondage. I slide into her slowly, pausing to feel the friction of her skin against mine. It's my scene. My trigger. My thing. She loves to be trussed up, and I love to see the inscription it leaves on her.

I kiss her once, twice, and then kiss along the rope patterns just below her neck. I start to thrust. Pull all the way out so that only the head of my cock is penetrating her. And then I drive deep. I do this over and over and over until Alice is bucking under me, muttering my name, dropping pleas and making bargains. She'd sign a pact with the devil if I fucked her just a little harder, and that knowledge makes me smile.

"Harder?" I ask, just to tease her. I can feel her cunt, gripping me like a humid, silken fist.

She nods and licks her upper lip. She's hardly ever aware that she does that, and she has no idea what it does to me.

I grab her a bit tighter and really start to move. All she needs, I give it to her. All she wants, I give it to her. She finds my face with her small, thin hands and begs me with her mouth for a kiss. I give it to her. I thrust my tongue into her mouth as I fuck her. She clamps herself around me, and the pleasure that floods my lower half steals my breath. It's my turn to say her name.

She flings her arms above her head, and I see the lines on her skin flow north with the motion. She's striped and crossed and dotted with the evidence of my control and I groan. Because seeing that evidence robs me of current control. I'm powerless against the unwound Alice. I'm humbled by her strength.

If someone tied me up and left me in the dark for hours, I'd lose my mind. I grind my hips back and forth, still buried deep inside her. That friction makes her pussy clench me harder, makes her breath come faster.

I trap her wrists above her head with one hand. Slide my free hand along her crosshatched flanks. I'm still rocking back and forth and the noise she's making tells me she's close—god, so close.

I give her mouth another kiss, her left breast another suck, another bite and then...I'm lost in her. Driving deep, following the call of my own orgasm. When she bucks up and I force her hands back, not giving her any room to move, that gesture seals the deal. Alice comes in a rapid-fire series of spasms.

I watch her face and when she opens those big brown eyes, she's never looked more lovely. Or more honest.

"Gabriel," she says again and that's that. I manage to bury myself in her three more times before I tip forward into my own release. I rest my head on the X on her flesh and listen to her heart.

MY PRETTY
PONY

D. L. King

He loved the feel of Elizabeth's naked cunt against his skin; leaving her wet, fragrant scent on his body; marking him as hers. Being much stronger, he wrestled her around, making sure his legs, chest, waist and arms were marked before settling down to drink from her, marking his face with her juices.

They liked having marathon sex sessions, rolling around in bed for hours on a Saturday, until they finally got hungry enough to get up, take showers, dress and go out for dinner. It was during one of these sessions when she managed to climb on his back, with legs thrown over his hips, biting and licking the back of his neck, that he got the idea. It just felt so right. He bucked up on his forearms and shins, raising her above the bed.

She sat him like a horse and wiggled. "I think all I need right now is a riding crop," she laughed. And before he could think about what he was saying, he blurted out, "Yes, that's exactly what you need."

She went still. "What?"

"Well, it'd be fun, don't you think?" He collapsed and rolled over to face her. "Don't you think it would be fun? Sort of an adult form of *horsey.*" He grabbed her by the waist and planted a quick kiss on her mouth. He lifted her off him and rolled off the bed. "Where do you want to eat?" he asked, on his way to the bathroom.

"I don't know. You decide. Hey, how come you get to shower first?"

"That's what happens when you're bigger and stronger."

"Yeah, well I guess all that hard work makes horses all stinky and sweaty."

It was a good sign, that horse remark. Maybe she didn't think it was all that weird, after all.

Bart was his own boss. He was a CPA and worked out of a home office. He was well organized, great with money and with time management. Elizabeth worked at an art gallery in the city. She loved her job but was sometimes envious of Bart for not having to wake up early every day or make the rush-hour commute.

It was one of those days.

He was sleeping all too peacefully. She gave him a shove and when he rolled over and looked at her, bleary eyed, she said, "Oh, did I wake you?" He grunted something and began to roll back over. "Since you're up, why don't you join me for breakfast?"

Grumbling, he rolled off the bed, put a robe on and stumbled after her into the kitchen. Elizabeth wasn't really a breakfast person but everyone said breakfast was important so she forced herself to eat something every day. Usually she only had coffee at home and then had breakfast at the gallery, but today she decided to make toast and peanut butter for both of them. As he drank his coffee and munched on food he didn't want, he realized he wouldn't be able to go back to bed when she left.

By the time he was fully awake, she was ready to leave. "There, that's better, isn't it?" She grinned and kissed him.

"I'm onto you, woman."

"Sometimes I just don't think it's fair, that's all. Why should I be the only one who has to get out of bed? It'll be good. You'll get a lot done. You'll see."

After she was gone, he poured himself another cup of coffee. Though a little pissed off to be up so early, he figured he could indeed get some work done. So he sat down at the computer in his shorts and robe and began searching for erotic equestrian sites.

A week later, in bed, he presented her with a black-leather riding crop and a pair of beautiful, black-leather riding boots.

With a curious half smile, she said, "What are these for?"

"I thought, maybe, we could play with them. Like, you know how I like it when you're on top, right? Maybe we could, like, play horse—or something." He wasn't sure this was going right. It wasn't unfolding the way he'd imagined it in his head.

"So, you want me to hit you with this?" She held up the riding crop. "On your butt? The boots are nice. Mind if I try them on?"

She seemed much more interested in the boots than the whole sexy, horsey thing, but she was always interested in shoes and boots. "Sure, that's what I got them for."

She leaned back against the pillows and pulled the right boot on. The sight of her, naked, legs spread, pulling on a leather boot forced a good-sized tear of precome from the tip of his cock. "How does it feel," he asked.

"It's good, I think. I just want to try the other one on, too." Once she'd gotten both boots on, she hopped out of bed to walk around in them. "Wow, these are nice. These aren't cheap, crappy boots. These are the real deal. I think I love 'em."

Looking at her standing by the bed, naked except for a pair of black leather boots, hands on hips, legs slightly spread, made his cock lurch forward like a divining rod. He climbed off the bed and handed her the crop. "Oh god, you are so hot." Down on his knees, in front of her, he ran his hands up the sides of the boots and buried his face in her pussy. He parted her lips and began to lick before grabbing her ass and trying to force as much of her as possible into his mouth.

He felt a light tap on his hip. "Hey horsey, I'll give you some sugar for a ride." He almost melted into a puddle in front of her but managed to get down on his hands and knees and whinny. It wasn't a very good whinny, but he supposed he could work on it.

She rested her hands on his shoulders, to balance herself, and lifted a leg over. The feel of her hot, wet pussy on the small of his back forced more precome from his cock but when she smacked his rear with the crop and said, "Giddyup!" he thought maybe he just might lose it right there.

She led him out of the bedroom and into the kitchen before dismounting. She poured herself a glass of water and leaned back down to him, a cube of sugar in the palm of her hand. It wasn't what he'd been thinking of in terms of *sugar*, but his lips took it from her, nevertheless.

"Okay, I can see where this could be fun," she said. "Want some water?"

He shook his head.

"All right then." She climbed onto his back again and said, "Back to the bedroom, Flicka," giving him a little smack with the crop. Once back in bed, she took control and rode him hard, keeping her new boots on the entire time.

* * *

Thinking back to that day, Bart realized it was the most exciting sexual adventure of his life, at least, up to that point. It wasn't just the sex, which was definitely hot, especially with her on top; it was the whole idea of her embracing his fantasy, or at least giving it a chance. Seeing her in those boots, remembering her wielding the crop during their trip to the kitchen. He'd never realized how hot the whole pony play fantasy was until he'd gotten a chance to make it a reality.

He still wasn't sure whether Elizabeth was just trying to please him, or if she was as turned on by it as he was. All he knew was that they spent a lot of time looking at Internet sites and equine paraphernalia, both together and, at least on his part, alone. They bought some gear, things like rubber bits, bridals and halters with reins and horseshoe mitts and boots. Elizabeth was getting pretty adept with the riding crop and so Bart bought her a few more, along with a dressage whip.

Elizabeth balked at the whip. She said she didn't want to hurt him, but she began practicing with it and, after a while, got up the courage to try using it on him. It seemed to transform her and after a while, it became an extension of her hand. He loved the feeling of it on his back, buttocks and thighs and he especially loved the little red marks it left on him, even though they quickly faded. Just feeling the little stings as he pranced around the house on hands and knees excited him like nothing else.

Elizabeth called those times his training sessions. She'd guide him through the house, sometimes riding on his back and sometimes walking beside him, using the whip or the crop, finally driving him back to the bedroom, where she'd take control again and fuck him senseless.

Bart was sure he'd reached the pinnacle of happiness. He couldn't imagine things getting better. How could they? Then, one day, he and a couple of friends went to a baseball game. He left the house late morning and didn't get home until just before dinner. Waiting for him, at the door, he found his horse-shoe mitts, bridal, bit and halter and a note, telling him to get ready and meet his rider in the den. Thankful he hadn't brought anyone home with him, he dutifully took off his clothes and transformed himself into Flicka (the name had stuck) and made his way, on his hands and knees, to meet Elizabeth.

The first thing he noticed, of course, was her booted feet and legs. Allowing his vision to travel upward, he saw that she was wearing a pair of camel-colored jodhpurs—but with a difference. The crotch was completely open. They were almost like chaps, but the rich wool jodhpurs had been beautifully tailored that way. It seemed she, too, had been busy on the Internet.

He whinnied and snorted and sidestepped closer to nuzzle her pussy. His tongue snaked out around his bit to give her a few licks before she smacked him lightly with her crop and backed up. "You have to see the whole package," she said.

He whinnied again and whined just a little, but dutifully looked up. She was dressed in an English riding outfit: leather riding boots; jodhpurs; white, tailored show shirt; black jacket and helmet. She held a pair of black-leather riding gloves in her hand, along with the ever-present riding crop. She was a goddess. He couldn't help it; he collapsed onto his butt, sat down and just gazed up at her. "What did I ever do to deserve you?" he said, around the bit in his mouth.

"Bad horsey, if you keep talking, I'm going to have to change your name to Mr. Ed—and he wasn't at all sexy. And horses don't sit down like that."

Bart got back on his hands and knees and Elizabeth approached him. Reaching down, she unclipped his bit. This time, she pulled his head against her cunt, pushing his nose into her slit, allowing him to bury his tongue inside her before he began licking and sucking her already dripping sex.

When he wrapped an arm around her thighs, she smacked his rear hard with the crop. "Ponies can't wrap a leg around something, and they can't effectively stand on three legs." He put his arm back down and Flicka snorted against her cunt, teasing it with his nose and tongue again.

"That's better," she said, letting him lick and suck her a little more. "I have a present for you, but it's far away and we'll have to ride there." She replaced the bit in his mouth and clipped it to the side of his halter.

Flicka whinnied and nodded his head up and down. Thoroughly wet, both from her own juices and his mouth, she climbed onto his back and rubbed herself against his bare skin. She took his reins and guided him through the house, first to the kitchen for a sugar cube and then around the living room—twice—down the hall and into the bedroom where she dismounted and retrieved a wrapped box from the dresser.

"Don't worry, I'll open it for you," she said. He watched as she ripped the paper off and opened the box. Inside was a shiny, stainless-steel butt plug with a beautiful, long, brown horsetail attached to it. "I think this works better when you're standing on two legs," she said. "Do you want to try it on?"

Though his eyes had gotten big, he nodded his head again and snorted. Up to this point, Bart had only had Elizabeth's finger in his ass, so the plug was a little scary, but the tail was so beautiful, he really wanted to try it.

Elizabeth decided it would be a good idea if he could talk, in case he needed to, so she removed his bit again and had him bend over the bed. "Let me know if I hurt you, baby," she said.

Using plenty of lube, she teased him open with her finger and played inside him until he was relaxed and opened enough to try the butt plug. It took a bit of effort and Bart gasped as the largest part of the plug slid past his sphincter, but once it was fully in him, he said it didn't hurt at all.

Elizabeth had gone all out and gotten a special plug, with an elbow that angled up and away, so the tail would sit like a real horse's tail. As he moved he noticed first the sensation of the plug moving inside him, which made him hard, and the feeling of the tail brushing against the backs of his knees, which made him even harder. The whole experience threatened to make him lose control altogether.

She led him to the mirror so he could admire himself as she stroked his hard cock and fondled his balls. "What do you think, baby?"

"Oh, my god. This is amazing," he replied, looking at himself from all angles. The whole *I'm a horse and can't talk* thing went right out of his head, but she didn't seem to mind. They had gone past the first game, into a whole new game; this one even more sexual than the last. He held his hands out. "Please?" he asked.

She removed the horseshoe mitts and he enveloped her in his arms. As her hands explored his ass, the plug and the tail, he ran a hand slowly down her back, over her butt and between her legs to finger her exposed cunt. It was obvious that the whole thing had turned her on, as she was even wetter than before.

Bart wondered what it would feel like to fuck her while the plug was in his ass. It was an imperative; he needed to know.

He walked her back against the side of the bed and laid her down. As he bent over her, kissing her, he could feel the plug slide inside him. It made his cock jump in her hand and he felt her smear his precome over the head of his shaft. She slid back farther onto the bed and he followed her, kneeling over her. The opening in her pants was just the right size and in just the right place to allow him access without her having to remove the jodhpurs.

He guided himself into her and his muscles squeezed against the plug as the tail draped over the backs of his legs. Every move excited him more. Every thrust sent an electric current through him, threatening to tip him over the edge, but he held on, making it that much more intense. He felt Elizabeth panting hard under him. He could feel the walls of her pussy squeezing his cock as she guided his hand to her clit. When he began to finger her, he could tell she was close to coming, but she wrapped her hand around the base of the tail and pushed down, prodding his prostate and sending him right over the edge. He lost all control as he bucked out his orgasm against her, not knowing if she'd been able to climax.

He must have looked upset, when they parted, lying on their sides, gazing at each other. "What's wrong," Elizabeth asked. "Are you okay?"

"I'm so selfish," he moaned. "I didn't make you come. I'm so sorry but I couldn't stop."

"Are you kidding?" Elizabeth replied. "I don't think I've ever come so hard before. I could feel that plug in you with every thrust. It was amazing! And when you came, it was like you were a machine, like you were in overdrive. Feeling you pound against me while the orgasm took you pushed me over a second time. Wow. Just, wow. I think there's more to explore here."

He kissed her. "Wow is right." A minute later, he said, "Honey, do you think you can take the plug out now?"

"I don't know," she replied. "I might want to keep you as a pony a little longer."

He gave her a look.

"Oh, all right. Besides, I'm hungry and you have to go out and pick up dinner. You'd probably scare the pizza guy, if he saw you like that, and we really like that pizza!"

MONTHLY

Vida Bailey

The basement was coldish. Colder when she was naked. Especially when she was cuffed on a length of chain too short to reach the bed. It was a good bed. Not what you'd expect to find in this dungeon, with its one small, high skylight and bare walls and floor. A soft mattress, with deep burgundy sheets and pillowcases. The thick duvet was the same shade, but dotted with tiny white flowers. She loved it. She wanted to be huddled underneath it, her body's heat accumulating until she was warm and cozy again. Her knees hurt on the concrete but her butt was too tender to sit on that hard floor. She pulled on the chain, but there really wasn't any give.

Very little of the noise filtered down from upstairs. He'd told her he was having a cocktail party. She hadn't realized it would be this weekend, and that she wouldn't be invited. She wondered if it was a work party, or one of the ones she featured at. Not as a guest, as entertainment. Last month, the party had been quite exclusive. Only five guests. Her memories of the evening were interrupted by the sound of footsteps on the basement stairs. She recognized his step. Measured, casual, confident. The lock clicked and the door swung open. He could have oiled the hinges, but she suspected he loved the creaking sound.

"God, these people are so boring." A work do, then. Ben's other friends were anything but boring. She heard the leather chair in the corner adjust to his weight. She didn't look up at him yet. The noise of his zipper sliding down was loud in the room. "You look a treat, there, Katie, chained to the ground with your bruised ass in the air. Sore, is it?" She nodded. "What's that?"

"Yes, Sir. It's sore. I'm cold, too."

"Complaints? Oh, Katie. What a disappointment. Perhaps I'll have to take your bed away completely to make you appreciate how good I am to you." She was alarmed to feel her eyes prickling at the suggestion. How long had she been chained like this? "Ah, Katie, it's a pity I have to host this party. They'll miss me shortly, so I don't have the time I'd like to teach you a lesson. You need another lesson, don't you, Kit?" She felt his eyes roam down her spine, over her painted behind. There was no mirror here, but she could feel the bruises blooming on her skin. "Yes, I think so. If I had time, I'd tape those cheeks open and punish that bad little hole with the strap. Your sensitive little asshole gets tender so quickly, doesn't it?"

"Yes, Sir."

"Makes it sting so much more when I fuck it, even though the cold lube on your hot, red skin feels so good, hmm?"

"Yes, Sir." She heard him stand and walk closer, heard the soft rasp of his hand moving on his cock.

"It's a pity, Katie, that I don't have time to open you up right, and fuck your ass. Kit, someone might come looking and find you on all fours in here, with your hole stuffed. Richard's here, maybe it would be him. I wonder if he'd fire you or promote you, what do you think?" Ben's hands ran the length of her spine. He stroked over her cheeks and parted them. He squeezed her cunt, and her juice ran over his fingers. "Oh, such a wet little slut. You'd like it if he joined in, wouldn't you?" Katie groaned and arched toward Ben as best she could. For a second the noise upstairs grew louder and she tensed, but the basement door stayed shut, no more footsteps. Ben pushed her lips apart with his thumbs and sank into her cunt. "This will have to do, for now." He reached beneath her and pinched her sore nipples with strong fingers. He fucked her with short, tight thrusts, the kind that made him come. It didn't last very long. He pounded into her with efficiency, reached around to put his fingers in her mouth and came fast. He loosened the chain and pulled her to her knees to clean their juices off his cock. "Don't get the bed too messy." He patted her cheek and whisked out the door, back to the party. He left the smell of his aftershave behind, mingling with champagne fumes and the musk of his semen between her legs. She crawled into the bed and fell asleep.

In her dreams she heard music and laughter and the hum of a busy party. Then it changed into someone screaming her name. She floated out of sleep, alarmed to hear the voice still calling, frantic and scared. Through bleary eyes, she saw her colleague Malory kneeling in front of her, calling her. She sat up, letting the cover fall from her and revealed her nakedness and her chained wrists. Malory screamed again.

"Kate! Are you okay? Did Ben do this? Oh god! Oh god, is there a key?" She rattled at the cuffs, staring at Katie's breasts in abject horror.

"Malory, no, wait, wait."

"It's okay, we can get you out of here, there're too many people here for him to do anything, you'll be safe!" Katie rolled her eyes inwardly. She could feel subspace Katie backing away,

and office Katie slipping back into her heels. She struggled to
be kind.

"Seriously, Malory, of all the explanations you could go to,
you choose to believe my boyfriend—your boss—is a psychotic
abductor who's going to kill us at his own cocktail party?"
Malory's mouth dropped open.

"What?"

Katie patted her hand.

"This is consensual. I want to be here. This is something
we…do, about once a month. Ben and I are more than a little
kinky, that's all. There's really nothing to worry about." Malory
continued gawping. Katie could see wheels whirring in her head.
"Malory, I have a horrible feeling you're about to say something
about Stockholm Syndrome. Please don't do that. I'm guessing
I'm the first person you've met who's come out to you as kinky?"
Malory got up off the mattress and brushed the creases from
her LBD.

"Please stop saying 'kinky,' Kate. As a matter of fact, no, I
haven't encountered anything like this before. And I have to tell
you I never would have expected this of you. I'm shocked."

"Don't worry, Malory, that's perfectly understandable.
Don't feel bad about it." Ben's smooth voice came from the
doorway. Malory whirled around, quite literally clutching her
pearls. Ben's smile was gentle, but Katie could see that he was
struggling not to tease his flustered colleague. "Revelations
like this can be shocking, if you're new to them. Perhaps you'd
like to sit down in my chair, and I'll have Katie show you how
much fun it can be?" Katie rested her forehead on her knees. It
wouldn't have been the first time she'd had her face between a
woman's legs as they spread them on the leather of that chair,
but she didn't usually have to discuss accounts with their owner
come Monday morning. Malory's horror, however, increased

tenfold. If Ben's suggestion had sparked a smidgen of interest, she pushed it right back down that instant.

"Ben! I'm going to go now!" She backed around him in a small circle and Katie heard her heels skip up the stairs when he started up after her.

"A quick word, Malory."

Katie flopped back into her bed and pondered. *If I was Malory, would I tell everyone? Or would I manage a little discretion?* She knew Ben was nothing if not persuasive. Ugh. This could be so messy. She imagined Malory backing up against the chair, letting Ben push her dress up her thighs, spreading them over the arms, pulling her knickers away from her sticky, shocked pussy. She imagineed what it would be like to have Ben's peremptory hand in her hair, pushing her forward into Malory's eager, open vulva. She didn't consider herself bi, but she did love to be made to do unpalatable things. Well, unpalatable was the wrong word in this case. Though...*Malory.* She considered the fact that Ben only hosted these parties to annoy her. Or torment her. Look at him, her career in potential tatters and he had her thinking about going down on Malory Smithson instead of coming up with a strategic plan. Being chained up in a cellar, covered in cum, was not conducive to strategic planning, she realized. Curse Malory for messing with her cumwhore weekend. Was being locked safely in a basement a couple of days a month really too much to ask? Katie laughed at herself cheerlessly and felt the beginnings of a serious funk begin to settle over her.

It was a couple of hours before Ben came back. He found her lying on her back, staring at the ceiling.

"All right, Kit?"

She looked over at him, eyes large.

"Ben, that was...bad. Do you think I should give all this

up?" He slipped his shoes off and got onto the bed behind her, lifting her onto his lap. He stroked her hair with a light, soothing touch.

"You could do that, Katie, though I'm not sure where that would leave me. The question is, do you really want to? Give up this thing that you get so much from, and that doesn't cause any harm to anyone else?"

She nuzzled into him, the smell of his aftershave, his skin under the dress shirt and jacket. When he put it like that…

"No. No, Sir, I don't."

"Good." He reached for the lube, the strap and the crop, and lined them up beside her on the bed. "I'm so glad."

DOING IT
BY THE BOOK

Tilly Hunter

I felt a bit silly, to be honest. It was a ridiculous position to be in. I'd expected the usual: spread-eagled on the bed with wrists and ankles tied to the corners. But Rob had read fast. I'd got him the book for his birthday, a bit of naughty amongst the sensible stuff he could show the family. *Get Your Kink On: A Beginner's Guide.* We weren't exactly beginners, but all my hints at doing something more adventurous had gone unheeded. But a guidebook, now that he could relate to. He's a techie. Instruction manuals are bedtime reading.

But my initial thrill when I'd realized I was finally getting something different was wearing off. My ankle cuffs were tied to the top bar of the headboard, pulling my legs up in the air over my head. Wrists were, as usual, tethered to the corners of the bed. My pussy was utterly exposed and it should have been the fulfillment of my long-held fantasies. But all I could think about was the way the position squashed all my flab up under my thighs and gave me triple chins. The muscles behind my knees were starting to ache.

"The position allows the Dominant to perform oral sex, or, should the submissive require chastisement, to administer punishment to the buttocks and thighs with the hand or an implement."

Oh god, he was actually reading from the text. And although the book was full of good ideas, it managed to convey them in a dry manner more appropriate to a computer programming manual. Rob was reading from Chapter Two: Basic Bondage for Sex and Dominance. The fancy stuff came in Chapter Three: Bondage for Decoration and Art. I knew. I'd already speed-read the book, careful not to bend the pages back, before wrapping it for him.

"The Dominant may also be able to perform intercourse, either vaginal or anal, although this requires a high degree of upper leg strength."

"Honey, perhaps I should admit that I've already read it," I said it. "So you don't need to say it all out loud."

"Oh, sorry," he said. "I wasn't reading it to you, I'm just making sure I cover everything. I won't be performing anal intercourse though so don't worry about that." He carried on the muttered monotone, *"The position does, however, inhibit access to the submissive's mouth."*

Oh Rob, I'm not worried, I said to myself. I'd never had anal, not with him or anyone else and Rob had made it clear the thought of back-door action was a turn-off for him. Ho hum, you can't have it all. At least he was trying with the bondage.

He'd lined up an array of equipment as if he was setting up a science experiment. Some we already had, a couple of vibrators, a soft blindfold. Some he'd actually ordered new without telling me. That was a first. A good sign. A wand vibrator, a gag, a spanking paddle. He seemed to be taking everything on board at once. But did he really have to lay it out like he was in a lab?

I lifted my head to let him draw the straps of the blind-fold over it and moaned softly. I couldn't see the rolls of flab anymore. Or the line of apparatuses. I felt his mouth on my pussy and breathed hard as his tongue flicked over my clit. But he was gone far too soon and all that was left was a breeze from the window cooling the dampness he'd created.

"Yes, the book's quite right. Good access for oral sex. Now let's see about the chastisement. Have you been a naughty girl, Sarah?"

"Oh yes, I'm a very naughty girl making you do this to me." I played along but I was just going through the motions. I didn't feel like a naughty girl desperate for a spanking. Even if I usually was.

I felt the paddle rubbing on the back of my thigh and tensed in anticipation. He'd skipped to Chapter Five: Erotic Punishment.

Most Dominants like to introduce the instrument of punishment to the submissive by rubbing it over the area to be beaten in order to sensitize the skin and/or having the submissive kiss or suck the instrument.

The paddle moved to my mouth and I pecked its cool surface before Rob took it away again. I was trying to follow his move-ments by the sound of his knees brushing on the duvet and the feel of the mattress rocking beneath my back. But the spank of the paddle on the back of my thigh still took me by surprise. I'd been mid-inhale when it landed, making me gasp out what little air was in my lungs and gulp for more. He'd only ever spanked me with his hands before. I wouldn't say this was harder, but it was different. The unvarying cool hardness of a leather pad rather than the growing warmth of flesh and the variance of fingers, palm, heel of the hand.

Just as I was really getting into it, starting to squeal, thighs tensed and fingers clenched, he stopped.

"You seem to like that," he said, running a finger through my now-wet pussy. Wet despite his dry, methodical approach.

I didn't want to have to give feedback on every little thing right now. Like it was some kind of psychological profiling questionnaire. "Yes," I murmured. "I like that."

"I'm going to try the gag out now and then some of these other new things I got."

My moan was one of frustration. I couldn't explain now, in this position, exactly how he was getting it so wrong. I wanted to cry. I felt the ball gag at my lips and parted them to let it in. He buckled it firmly into place. I gave in to being his science experiment. I realized it was part of us, our relationship. We'd met at work. I wrote the words that sold our company's wares— tantalizing descriptions that made people desperate to buy into the sophisticated lifestyle a new sofa would bring them. He made sure people could actually buy them, that our website was running as it should, our online security up to date, our ordering system functioning. Now, he was just doing his technical thing, while I longed for poetry. For emotional connection. For a submission I would feel in my soul.

He slid a dildo inside me. The spanking had already made me slippery. He held it there while he fidgeted and fiddled with something else. Plugging something in. Which could only be that new magic wand vibrator he'd bought. I was quite excited about that. We'd always shied away from the price.

Its motor sounded totally different from our other vibrators. A low hum. He pressed it to my clit and it thrummed through me, barely there. He turned it up. Fuck me, it was power-shower intense, if you know what I mean. And it had more to come. As I squirmed as far as my restraints would let me and squealed uncontrollably, he turned it up again. It was right on the edge of a stimulation so intense it would be intolerable. Within seconds

I came in an orgasm that clenched every muscle and had me screaming around the gag. But, deep down, I wasn't satisfied.

We discussed the results of the experiment later over a glass of Rioja. "You seem to have enjoyed pretty much all of it," he said.

"Yes, I guess I did."

"But?"

"It's hard to explain. I wish I could create some kind of collage of all the crazy, kinky thoughts and images that go through my head. I liked it all, I liked the position and the spanking and the gag and the wand vibe. But overall, it felt very mechanical. Like you were just following the instructions from the book instead of being actually there with me, in the moment."

How could I say that it was just the way he did it? That he hadn't seemed like the natural Dom I wished he could be? That I wanted him to do a Superman-style transformation from rational techie into teasing, inventive fuck-god.

"If you can't tell me, maybe you should show me," he said.

"What do you mean?"

"You do it to me. Just once. An experiment for you to show me what you mean. I'm not saying I really want you to, but if that's what it takes for me to understand, then you show me."

Ah, that's the reason I love him in spite of everything. He's such a reasonable kind of guy. He made it sound like the perfect solution, easiest thing in the world for me to do a 180-degree switch in my psyche.

"Just don't be going near my ass," he added.

"Um, okay."

So that's how I found myself sitting on the end of the bed with Rob tied in the position I'd been in. I'd been very careful with him, following the book's advice: *Most men are not as flexible as women and may find this position difficult to hold for any period of time. This can be alleviated by attaching the restraints above the knees instead of to the ankles to allow the legs to bend farther.* Not that I had the book out and open at that page. I'd prepared earlier, deciding what to do, and put the book back on the shelf. I noted with annoyance that he had no rolls of flab, just a slight fold across the belly button.

"Comfy?" I asked.

"I wouldn't say that. But I'm okay for now."

"Enjoying it?"

"Pass."

I ran my fingernails down the tender back of his thigh and he squirmed. I did it harder. I'd expected red marks straight away, but it wasn't until I'd been raking his skin for a couple of minutes that it began to redden. I brushed my nails lightly up the underside of his still-limp cock, making it jerk. Bending my mouth to it, I tongued it inside, sucking as it hardened and swirling my tongue around the head as it emerged from his foreskin. He moaned and I drew back, letting his now-hard shaft drop from my lips.

"You seem to be getting aroused darling," I said.

"Yes, I do."

"Is that because of, or in spite of, the fact that you're tied up?"

"In spite of. I think. My thighs ache."

"Oh, poor you. You'll just have to be a man and take it, I'm afraid. There's no way I'm letting you go just yet now that I have you here all helpless and vulnerable." I really did feel a visceral stab of power go through my torso and into my cunt. I wanted to toy with him and tease him and use his body for my own amusement. It made me wish I'd tied him in a position in which I could fuck him, or at least get my pussy to his mouth.

"I'm going to blindfold you." I drew the elastic bands of

the blindfold over his head and positioned it. "Can you see anything?"

"No."

"Not even down here?" I waved my hands down low along the sightline of his nose.

"No, not anywhere." I guessed his nose was a different shape than mine. Maybe it was that old football injury that squashed it a bit. I leaned in between his knees and kissed his mouth. He didn't expect it and didn't pucker up to meet me until I'd already pressed my lips to his. It made me smile to see him still reaching his face up to me as I moved away. He groaned as he let his head fall back on the pillow.

I tongued his cock again, just enough to keep him hard. I wanted him to enjoy himself. Partly so he wouldn't call a halt to the whole thing and partly to try to show him how pleasurable this could be, how good he could make me feel when the roles switched again. But he had to feel the paddle too. To gain an understanding of *the instrument,* as the book put it, and realize the difference between a palm and an inanimate object that never grew hot and stinging and tired.

I brought it to his lips, then turned it to push the end into his mouth. He whimpered and pressed his head back into the pillow, but I thrust it in farther, not letting him get away. "Suck it," I said. He stopped fighting and formed his lips around it. It was an awkward shape and his sucking gave off messy, slurping noises. It made my pussy pulse.

I drew it out and again he tried to follow it with his lips to the point where his shoulders would go no farther against the bonds. I brought it down on his asscheek, hard. He gasped and jerked. "This is just the beginning, honey," I said. "You can take a lot more than that."

I paddled the same spot, building up a rapid rhythm. I figured he was the kind of guy who would like a pattern to the blows, a beat he could prepare for mentally. I could have toyed with him more. Switching sides, rubbing the paddle's soft surface against him and beating him unexpectedly. But I'd reached a point where I was really worried he was going to tell me to stop. We hadn't taken the book's advice. Chapter One: Safety and Preparation. Page One: Safewords. This was just practice. Rob was not my submissive. If he said "stop" it meant "stop."

My imagination wandered as I beat him and his butt started to glow. He was moaning, but it sounded more like arousal than pain. His ass was on display and the position parted his cheeks, showing me his dark hole. I'd never wanted to invade it before, but there it was and it clenched as he tensed his pelvic muscles with each blow. The passage from the book ran through my mind, *The Dominant may also be able to perform intercourse, either vaginal or anal.* There was a whole chapter on anal later. I'd been drawn to the discussion of butt plug sizes—*Too small, large and too large,* it joked. I wouldn't go against his wishes on something like this, but part of me wanted to thrust at least a finger in there.

His moans were rising in pitch and he was starting to pull on the restraints. I stopped paddling him before he had to ask me to. This wasn't about him begging for mercy because it was too much; it was about taking him to a place where it was still pleasurable.

I ran my fingers over his tender flesh and he gasped at the change of sensation. I grasped his shaft and pumped it in my hand, making sure the tingle in his skin would be associated with pleasure for his cock. He fought against the ropes holding his knees in place to thrust his hips in time to my hand. When I licked the tip of his cock as I stroked, he started groaning with every breath. I noted with amusement how tightly clenched his fingers were around the bars of the headboard. I could get into this. I wondered if Rob could get into this. If, perhaps, he was already getting into this.

"I'm going to gag you now, just so you can get a feel for it," I said. "Just for a moment, then I'll take it off, okay?"

"Okay." His voice was low and breathy.

He opened his mouth when he felt the ball at his lips, and I fastened it snugly but not too tightly. He could probably have pushed it out, but I didn't want to give him jaw ache. Not in the way it had given me jaw ache. The way that I had relished. I went back to his cock and took it as deep into my mouth as I could, pumping my lips over him and sucking him to the edge of coming. I liked the way his moans had changed, the gag muffling them and making them all throaty.

Licking off the tip of his cock, I asked, ever considerate, "Would you like me to take the gag back off again now?"

He didn't answer for a moment. Then he shook his head.

"No?" I said, surprised.

He shook his head again and grunted as close to the word, "No," as it allowed him.

That shake of the head did something to me. It made me want to slide onto his cock and fuck him senseless. Instead, I plugged in the wand vibe and turned it on. He tensed as he heard it. I wondered what he thought. That I might leave him there while I made myself come? That I might shove it against his ass?

I shifted his balls upward and pressed it to the base, against his perineum. He managed to squeeze out the word, "Fuck," around the gag while his whole body bucked. The vibe was only on low. I held it there while I sucked his cock hard and deep. When his body relaxed and he started rocking to my rhythm, I edged the motor up a little. He was breathing hard but made no more attempts at speech. I could feel the vibrations through my mouth. It was a powerful little thing. His cock grew and hardened just before he pumped out the biggest load I have ever had to swallow.

I took the gag out straightaway, but it was a while before he recovered his wits enough to speak. I removed the blindfold and he just gazed at me as I released his legs and untied his wrists. He let his limbs lie where they fell, making no attempt to move them for himself.

"You seem to have got into that in the end," I said, leaning over to kiss him and run a thumb up his jaw.

He made a caveman grunt.

"I want to sit on your face while you lick my clit until I come," I added.

"Mmm-huh." It sounded positive, so I straddled his head and lowered my pussy onto his mouth.

It took another bottle of Rioja before he put the experience into words.

"I didn't expect it to be like that," he said. "I thought it was just a physical thing for me to feel what it was like to be tied up like that and spanked and played with. But it was so much more than that. You sucking my cock helped, obviously, but when you made me suck the paddle and then teased about whether I could take the spanking and how helpless I was, I…well all I can say is it really turned me on."

"It turned me on too, seeing you like that and having you at my mercy. I think I could be a lot more wicked, given the chance."

"You see, even that, you saying that now, you've made my cock twitch."

"This is an unexpected result," I said. "Are we going to have to take it in turns to be tied up?"

"I think we might have to. And, oh god, I don't quite know how to say this. I'm scaring myself. You know what I said about not going near my ass?"

"Yes." I raised an eyebrow.

"When I was tied with my legs up like that and my ass was all open and exposed and every now and again your fingers would brush past my crack or I felt the draft from the paddle across it...I liked it. Do you think maybe you could push a finger in sometime, just as an experiment?"

Hell yes. I felt my throat tighten just to hear him confess this and to imagine the prospect of entering his body. "Yes," I said. "I think I could try that. Perhaps we should both reread Chapter Eight. But remember, it's my turn next."

"It is," he said. "And I already have a few ideas. I'm going to check over Chapter Six first."

I knew Chapter Eight: Anal Training. But I had to run upstairs and pull the book off the shelf to remind myself of Chapter Six: Collars and Clamps.

SEX PARTY
MAGIC

Kristy Lin Billuni

Y ou look perfect. Daddy has surprises for you."

Ceci and Eddie kissed their first really girlfriendy kiss, the romantic greeting of lovers who expect to be kissed, when Eddie arrived Wednesday evening in a black T-shirt and black jeans. She carried a small black duffel and had buzzed Ceci from the street. They now stood in her doorway, Eddie's smile bursting.

"Come in, come in. Can I make you a drink?"

"No, I want my wits about me. And you can stop drinking too." Eddie removed a glass from Ceci's hand.

She shook that off but didn't understand it. Weren't they going out to play? "So this is my place. Oh, that's right, you were up here already. Jeeze, I don't even really remember that."

"I will never forget it." Eddie glanced at Ceci's tits and moved closer to run both hands up and down the sides of her torso. "Mmm...you dressed just as I wanted you." Ceci wore her new black slip-dress, a matching slingshot panty, and black heels.

Eddie looked down between their close bodies at Ceci's feet.

"Nice shoes." She lifted Ceci's skirt and approved the panties with a nod. She ran a thumb over each nipple, through the slip-dress's thin fabric. She smiled at the rings she'd placed there and flipped one up and down again. A tiny zip shot through Ceci's body.

They kissed again. Eddie's hands played with Ceci's hair and settled on the crown of her head. She pressed her down in that quiet way that boys use to hint for a blow job. Ceci remembered it from high school and had sought it out in porn. Eddie conjured make-believe in the real world. Maybe she had caused this freakish San Francisco snowfall. Submission and snow—these things she thought she despised turned beautiful around Eddie.

Ceci dropped with enthusiasm to her knees to face Eddie's unbuttoned fly. When had she managed that? She wore boy undies—*tighty-whities*, Ceci had always called them.

She looked up at Eddie for permission and then burrowed her nose into the opening. She nuzzled through cotton folds into fleshy ones and found Eddie's cock—rather, the clitoris she wielded like a cock. First, Ceci flirted with it, rubbing her nose into the space between inner and outer labia, breathing Eddie's musk.

Ceci realized the girth of it when she finally encircled Eddie's clit with her tongue. She let the whole thing swell in her mouth, sucked it, and pulled her lips from base to tip, up and down the shaft. She sucked Eddie's inner labia into her mouth too, adding padding and friction, length and width. Eddie's grip tightened in her hair, and Ceci smiled to herself.

This was old-fashioned butch-femme dyke sex. Eddie wasn't that much older than her, but she embodied a queer aesthetic that Ceci hadn't seen around in a long time. Were all the old-school butches taking testosterone these days?

Eddie fucked her face now, pushing deeper into her mouth. Ceci opened wider and felt the swollen clit strain toward her uvula. Eddie moaned and pressed hard on the back of Ceci's head, hips thrusting forward. Ceci reached out her tongue and lapped at Eddie's sopping cunt, testing the boundary for penetration. She wanted to get a finger in there.

Eddie's pelvis settled into Ceci's wide-open mouth, demanding deeper tongue and shoving her erect clit toward Ceci's throat. Ceci lifted her hand; one finger, two slipped easily into Eddie's hole and found her G-spot, throbbing and soggy. She tightened her lips around the clit and concentrated her sucking there while she pumped two fingers against the inner wall of Eddie's pussy. It gripped her fingers with a tight, insistent rhythm.

It didn't take long. She rocked her hips against Ceci's face while hot liquid flooded her wrist, her face and her tits. Eddie crumpled to the floor in front of Ceci. Ceci sat back and leaned on her arms, Eddie's cum smeared across her face. They smiled at each other.

"Didn't muss your dress too much did I, baby?"

Ceci inspected the clear liquid stain on the slip's scoop neck. "Just enough for me to smell you all night."

"Good. Do you have a good coat?" Eddie stood, buttoning her fly, all business again.

Exhilaration held Ceci behind Eddie on the bike. She squeezed Eddie, embracing her trim, boxy, leathered chest and pressing her cheek against her muscled shoulder. They sped down Hyde Street and across Market, passing the Pussycat Lounge in a blur. SoMa streets buzzed, even on a Wednesday night, with club kids queued around the perimeter of warehouses and leather men smoking outside black-painted bar fronts.

They whipped past the black-painted, wooden façade of a

corner bar, where the Sisters of Perpetual Indulgence glittered outside, huge sequined eyebrows arched, ostentatious habits flapping, collecting donations and stamping the arms of furry bear fags.

Ceci had heard of The House, a private home reputed for its sex parties and fully functioning dungeon. She even knew which Dolores Park Victorian hosted the infamous parties, so when Eddie parked on the sidewalk in front of it, her heart fluttered.

She hopped off the bike and wedged her skull out of the helmet. Eddie removed her black duffel from the bike's saddlebags and locked the helmets to the bike. She placed a hand on Ceci's wrist, stopping her from heading toward the house. "Follow me."

She liked the way Eddie's rough hand gripped her wrist, but she surprised Ceci by leading them to cross away from The House. A little alley jutted toward Market from the other side of the street. The homes that lined it looked expensive. Eddie pulled her around its first curve, out of the streetlamp's reach, and whispered, "Turn around."

Ceci's breath quickened. If Eddie fucked her here, some onlooker might call the police or something. She felt Eddie's body against her backside, and her arms reached around Ceci's body to her throat. Then Eddie kissed her shoulder, using her chin to move the coat's furry collar out of the way, and wrapped a leather strap across her Adam's apple. She heard a click, and Eddie checked the collar's snug fit.

"This is your collar. You'll wear it when we play." Eddie breathed gravity into the moment, rested her hand on Ceci's head, and corrected her to bow it. "Now, let's go to the party."

In the white light of the foyer, Ceci saw the tiny chain and key around Eddie's neck and touched the nape of her own to discover that she was indeed padlocked, with a tiny lock and clasp, into her collar.

She realized she felt safe in this predicament. Eddie took her responsibility as a top so seriously, but would she ever actually get to know the real Eddie—outside of this game?

Two friendly women, dressed garishly in satin corsets and long velvet dresses, ample bosoms spilling everywhere, greeted them and took their coats. The next room had two long tables with plates of food and plastic party cups. Eddie drove Ceci through this and the next room—full of men in black shirts and no pants—and out to a back porch, candlelit with a hot tub full of revelers. They skirted the splashing, chlorinated sexual soup and descended wooden stairs into the dungeon.

Ceci had never seen anything like it—all this effort for adult play, for sex. Every wall featured a different structure, furniture she half recognized from wandering at the Folsom Street Fair last fall. A sling swung empty on one wall. A nude woman hung listless on a black, wooden X-shaped cross facing the other wall. Her pinkened back contrasted with her smooth, white shoulders, neck and legs. A man stood a few feet behind her with a heavy-looking leather whip. Beside the door they had just come through stood a sort of construction worker's sawhorse, painted black. Two women, dressed in lacy black and burgundy as if for the midnight *Rocky Horror Picture Show*, straddled it, giggling and kissing.

Another horse-thing, bigger, like in men's gymnastics but padded with black leather, stood perpendicular to the opposite wall. A man in boxer shorts and leather wrist restraints slumped alone on it, cock in hand, watching the giggling girls.

They breezed through this room too and into a mazelike make-believe sexual playground. A basement room with extra walls and the sawdusty scent of new construction wound around several corners, each wall with another plaything, a kitchenette where two women prepared piercing needles, another cross just like the first one, and a cage. It was early, and the party, no doubt, was just getting started, but Ceci noticed over Eddie's shoulder that they'd picked up an audience.

Eddie stopped and held Ceci by the arms. "Don't pay attention to the looky-loos, Ceci. It's just you and me." But the looky-loos made her feel beautiful and sexy. Wasn't that the point?

"Yes, Daddy," Ceci heard herself whisper. Maybe Eddie's voice hypnotized her.

The other faces faded when Ceci focused. With a tip of her rigid jaw, Eddie indicated a tall, metal, old-fashioned medical table. "I want you to go stand in front of that table."

She walked across the cement floor, heels tapping, many eyes on her, and struggled to climb up onto the table. She lost her confidence a little, the climb feeling not-so-sexy, clumsy. But as soon as she settled her rump, Eddie materialized before her, smiling.

"It's too tall, isn't it?" Eddie said. Ceci's knees pointed at Eddie's chest. "For me, too. This won't do." She offered Ceci a hand. "Hop down from there, babe."

She managed a more graceful dismount, and they walked around the maze while Eddie considered her options. Ceci listened to Eddie's even breathing and felt her own heart beating. She tried her best to ignore the growing audience, but the shadowed faces, blinking eyes and grisly smiles distracted her and toyed with her vanity.

Eddie had stopped in front of a black, wooden frame, like a doorway that went nowhere. In each of its corners shone a bolted ring. They matched her nipple rings. Eddie pointed to the ground, and it took Ceci a moment to realize she meant for her to sit there. She lowered down onto her haunches, thankful for a break for her feet.

Out of her duffel, Eddie produced four leather and fur restraints. Ceci had seen this sort of thing before. In fact, she had a set that she and Jane had bought years ago. You could pick them up for fifty bucks in any novelty sex shop.

But Eddie made no cheesy boudoir jokes. With a serious brow and tight focus, she clipped one cuff to each ring on the black frame, and Ceci wondered if her wrists would reach that high. Eddie pulled a couple more things out of the duffel, stuffed something shiny into her pants pocket and something leather under her arm, zipped up, and tossed the black bag into the corner behind the frame. She turned to look down at Ceci.

Ceci felt a surge in her heart. Was this love or just sex or kinky performance art? She didn't even know Eddie, not really. They had spoken very few words to each other, but she had submitted to Eddie in ways she would never have bowed to Jane—to anyone. Eddie dazzled her and made her cunt throb. Half naked, vulnerable, on her knees, with onlookers, she felt stunning, more radiant than she'd ever felt before. Eddie's palm pressed against the back of Ceci's head until her cheek smashed into the top's denim crotch. She closed her eyes and inhaled.

Ceci hadn't yet seen that her collar also sported a steel ring in front, but now Eddie linked a finger through it and yanked her to her feet. "Stand there." She pointed at the wooden frame.

Ceci obeyed.

Eddie reached between her bare legs with a stick—a switch. She smacked both her inner thighs and said, "Spread your legs, baby."

Ceci spread her stinging thighs open.

"More."

Eddie wanted her ankles nearer to the restraints, but the wider she spread her legs, the shorter she got, and the more impossible it would be for her wrists to reach. Would she get in trouble for just telling Eddie what she thought? Would getting in trouble be fun?

She placed one foot up against each leather cuff, unsure of the rules.

Eddie buckled her feet to the frame, stood, took her wrists, and stretched Ceci's arms to their limits. "Tsk tsk," she clucked. "I want you to wear higher heels next week."

So that was how it worked. The top blames the bottom's outfit. The burn of Eddie's rebuke felt almost as sexy as the sting of the switch on her thighs. "Yes, Daddy."

"Stand still." Eddie went back to her duffel and pulled out a wad of rope. She then surprised Ceci by approaching the gathered crowd. A tall man, with a barrel chest in a ruffled peasant shirt smiled at Ceci.

His mustache widened and then twitched when he leaned forward for Eddie to speak into his ear. They whispered back and forth for several minutes and walked toward Ceci with matched stride. Eddie stood close in front of her while the man circled around behind her.

Eddie smiled, and her field of vision turned black.

The man blindfolded her with a soft, silky scarf, tied it tight, and smacked her ass. Ceci squirmed. She didn't want to have sex with this guy, at least not for free. Ridiculous costume, unattractive—did Eddie know him? How would she know him from Eddie if she couldn't see?

The stranger smacked her ass again, and Ceci made a face that must have betrayed her thoughts. Eddie's voice breathed into her ear. "You have to trust me, Ceci. I'm in charge here."

She exhaled at that. She would trust Eddie's dedication to this Daddy identity even if she didn't like this other guy. She would surrender to Eddie, to this scene, to sexual magic.

"Answer me!"

Ceci's breath quickened "Yes, Daddy. Thank you, Da—"

"Good. Raise your arms high," said the strange man.

She did, and her wrists cuddled into the furry restraints, which tightened, so she hung a little. "Good girl," came Eddie's voice. "It's just you and me now." Her heated breath disappeared from Ceci's ear, and she waited in the dark. So Eddie had just needed this guy's help to set it up? Ceci had strategized around sex before, but she'd never prearranged logistical assistance.

Eddie's preparation for this game pleased her. She couldn't help but play along. Apparently, Eddie didn't need her to like this rope-tying assistant; she just needed Ceci to accept him in his role.

The room grew quiet, and she searched for the sound of Eddie's gait, her voice. The sound of soles smacking cement, running, came at her, and a loud, thumping weight fell on her back, then again, and again. It brought with it a fuzzy stinging, and each blow felt heavier. She leaned forward in the soft fur of the restraints, but the tiny leather straps—so many of them!—found her again and again. Pain and pleasure washed over her. She shut her eyes in their silk cocoon and rested.

She lost track of time, and then Eddie leaned into her back, kissed her shoulder, and said, "Good, baby. Very good." She cut the straps of Ceci's dress and then peeled it off her body so that she stood almost naked, the slip around her waist like a cummerbund. Eddie kissed her hot, welted skin, on her shoulders, her neck, down her spine, in tiny kisses. She ran a calloused hand across the places that hurt worst. Ceci winced. She felt high and drowsy.

A plastic straw pressed against her lips. "Drink," said Eddie. She sipped a little water and realized her thirst for it. Then the straw and Eddie vanished, and Ceci waited in the dark silence again.

No longer anxious, she could feel, almost hear, a rustling in the crowd while she rested, enjoying the moment. She had submitted to Eddie's imaginary world and reaped a reward for it: sparkly, sexual magic.

Cold, sharp metal pointed into her ankle. Eddie's voice traveled up from below her. "Stay very, very still, now, Ceci."

She tensed her body and held her breath. The cold edge of a knife ran up her calf, around the back of her knee, and up her inner thigh. Eddie pressed its blunt edge against her pussy lips, through the widest swath of fabric in her slingshot panties. Hot bubbling rushed inside her.

"You like that, huh?" Eddie kissed her, hard, with lots of tongue. Ceci kissed back, her mouth open. Their chests and bellies pressed together.

Eddie pulled away, and her knife teased one nipple ring, lifting it and letting it drop, the sharp edge grazing the underside of her nipple. Then the same thing, other nipple. This was repeated, back and forth several times, and Ceci's excitement heightened.

Eddie disappeared again. Ceci dropped to the floor suddenly, scaring herself. Her wrists must have been cut loose without warning. Onlookers murmured.

She waited for Eddie, upper torso curled on the floor, legs spread wide, still bound at each ankle to the frame. She wanted to touch her clit but felt too exposed. A thin cloth draped over her, and then Eddie's body smothered hers, surrounded her, gathered her up and carried her through the mazelike room.

Eddie whispered to her while she walked. "Daddy's very pleased, very pleased, and she's going to reward you now." They came to rest on a soft bed. Eddie removed Ceci's blindfold to candlelight, and they were alone. Eddie curled up on the bed behind Ceci, spooning her, stroking her. "You did so good,

Ceci. Thank you." She played with the clasp of the collar.

Ceci purred, "Not yet, please, Daddy. I'm still yours." The fiddling ceased, and she could feel Eddie smiling. Their cuddle tightened, and Eddie kissed her neck and nibbled her ear. Her arms reached around to Ceci's wet pussy. Her fingers separated lips and slipped among folds, found her clitoris and stroked its length.

She moved around Ceci and situated her on her back. "I want you to come for Daddy now." She continued to stroke her clit, the rhythm increasing. Ceci shut her eyes and concentrated on the constricting muscles in her cunt and her whole pelvis. A finger squished inside and pumped into her G-spot, then plunged very deep, toward her cervix. Ceci moaned, and Eddie continued smooth, deep strokes. Ceci's body shuddered and tensed. Eddie stopped and leaned hard on her clit and her G-spot at once, and everything released. Air rushed into her mouth and down her throat, and she cried out. Eddie's fingers ran down her legs with a light touch. "That's my girl."

Ceci curled into a fetal position, and Eddie returned to their spoon. She removed the collar and whispered in her ear, "We can't sleep here, Ceci. It's time to go."

Snow fell while they hurried down the front steps of The House, Eddie's arm draped over Ceci's shoulders. Ceci stopped to tie her severed dress straps into clumsy bows at each shoulder and pull her coat's furry collar close around her when the cold air woke her from the dreamy state her first sex party had created.

The dark-blue morning sky brightened while they rode up the winding roads to Twin Peaks, where the giant, red-and-white antenna towered above them.

Eddie parked among cars with steamed-up windows and laughed while she helped Ceci with her helmet. "We should knock and ask if anybody has room for us. It's fucking freezing."

Ceci smiled and leaned her head against Eddie's chest. "I'm not cold," she sighed and indulged in her buzz. Eddie's arms wrapped around her and rocked her back and forth, gazing out over the city at dawn. The snow added billions of twinkles to the already sparkly skyline.

"I think I'm starting to like this town."

"I thought I hated it at first," Ceci said. "But, yeah, me too. I'm liking it, despite this crazy, cold, white stuff that's falling on it."

"Damnedest thing. Snow in California in summertime."

"Can I ask you a question, Eddie?"

"I don't promise to answer."

The eastern sky glowed neon pink now, though the arc of sky above and behind them still loomed dark. Ceci shuddered and asked, "Who was that guy? The one who tied me up?"

"He's a friend, Ceci. We can trust him. We'll play with him again. You'll like his slave girl, Elizabeth."

"He's a straight guy?"

"You can hardly call somebody as kinky as William straight, but yeah, he prefers women. I know him from Boston. He's been a mentor to me."

"I don't know if I can handle this whole submission thing with a man," she blurted and then added, "What kind of relationship is this, Eddie? Are we going to get into each other's lives or are we going to do this daddy-baby girl thing?"

"Is there a difference?"

Now Ceci quieted. This snow cooled anger and muffled secrets. She didn't want to fight with Eddie, not tonight when she felt so happy and tingly. "I think there is a difference. I think what we're doing is play and make-believe and not a part of the real world."

Eddie lifted Ceci's face to hers with a finger and kissed her. "What we're doing is very, very real."

"I don't even know your real name."

"Eddie is my real name."

"Your birth name? And what's your last name?"

"Would that make me more real?"

They watched the pink diffuse to orange and white stripes across the bay sky. Ceci's mind wandered back to the black wooden frame and the silk scarf. Her back still stung with painful heat. "No, don't tell me. I like it like this—like magic."

"Me, too."

THE OTHER SIDE
OF THE ROPES

Kathleen Tudor

The ropes on the young woman's body traced back and forth like a corset from the sub's upper arms to her wrists. "Pretty in pink," Madame Angelie said, "but not functional." The dom who had tied the knots looked at her in consternation, not daring to oppose her word, but clearly certain that he'd done good work.

"What do you mean?" he finally bit out, his tone properly respectful, if strained. *Good, the puppy is smart.*

"It's too loose. And your knot is in the wrong place." She waited to see how he would react to her vague statements; Angelie never bothered with doms who couldn't be respectful of her superior knowledge, and she would downright sink him if he treated her like a doormat just because she was female.

This one, however, showed promise. Tyson took a slow breath through his nose, examining the rope work. "How can you tell?"

"Experience," she said with a smile. Then she pointed. "Do

you see how the rope barely even dents the flesh of her arms, here? There are no veins in the outer arm to cut off with tight ropes. Care must always be taken, obviously, but the ropes are too loose, particularly for a flexible sub. And Tonya is a very flexible girl, aren't you, baby?" Tonya shrugged, a dark red flush appearing on her cheeks.

"And the knot?"

"You're paying attention," Angelie said, approving. "It's between her wrists. She can reach it." He looked stunned, so Angelie decided to prove it. "Tonya, escape," she said.

The young woman immediately twisted her arms within the bonds, stretching for the knot and finding it easily. A few plucks, and it was loose. But she didn't stop her bratty demonstration there. Instead, she shifted her shoulders back, putting enough slack in the arm bind that it slid from her upper arms and pooled on the floor behind her. A pretty pile of useless ropes; she could have escaped even without untying the knot.

Tyson crossed his arms, obviously irritated. "What's the point of this? She did that on purpose!"

"Not every sub wants to meekly fold herself into position and wait for your ropes," Angelie said, running a long fingernail down Tonya's arm. The girl was unattached, but she and Angelie played together sometimes, and Tonya liked to demo for some of Angelie's classes. "This one can be particularly bratty, but even the most apparently docile subs sometimes flex to expand their rope work, or wiggle when they're tied. You have to understand what they get out of it. The thrill of *trying* to escape. That extra jolt of pleasure when they're outmatched and unable…"

"Yes, Mistress Angelie," Tyson said. Respectful, yes, but not convinced.

"You want a sub, or a doormat?"

"I'm sorry?"

"Do you want a *sub*, who will let you *take* whatever control you can *earn*, or do you want a meek little piece of furniture who stays where you put her?"

He looked taken aback. "A well-trained slave—"

"Might not leave a little slack in the rope for her own comfort, but you don't get a well-trained slave just by asking for one. You have to know how to train them, and that means *making* brats like Tonya respect you." She spanked Tonya hard, and the girl grinned and waggled her ass for more. "And you have to know what you're working with. Some of those so-called submissives are just gluttons for punishment." She kissed Tonya on the cheek. "What time does the sitter expect you back, honey?"

"In an hour, Madame Angelie."

"Go on, then, get yourself changed and all respectable-like. Thanks for your help, baby." They exchanged a brief—if spicy— kiss, and Tonya vanished into the front half of the dungeon, where the dressing rooms and lockers were.

"Thank you for your time," Tyson said, putting out his hand to shake.

Angelie waved her hand through the air. It was true, the rest of the class had already gone while she kept Tyson back for a little bonus instruction, but he was one of the good ones, and the scene needed more of those. "If you're not in a hurry, we can continue to work on it," she said.

His brow furrowed in confusion and he turned in the direction Tonya had gone, his mouth slightly parted as if desperate to ask a question, but not sure which question he should be asking. It was hard for Madame Angelie not to laugh at him, but she bit her tongue—men like Tyson had their pride, and she wouldn't trample on his.

"Untangle your rope, honey. You can practice on me."

"On *you?*"

"I may have a reputation for not subbing, but a good top knows how it feels to be on the bottom. No getting any ideas— this is just a demo." She put her arms behind her back, clasping them together behind the full roundness of her ass, and turned so that Tyson could reach her arms.

"You have to know your bottom," she said. "Her limits. Her mindset. Her quirks. Before that rope even touches my skin, I want you to push my upper arms together. Be firm; see if you can feel out my flexibility." She had intentionally *not* stretched her arms toward each other when she'd put her hands behind her back. When Tyson laid his big, strong hands on her arms, she let him push her upper arms back toward each other, resisting only slightly. "That's good. But is it as far as I can stretch? If you're working with a new sub, ask her."

He made a sound of understanding and started to release her, but then his grip tightened on her biceps, and Angelie smiled. "*Can* you go farther?"

"Why yes, baby, I can." He harrumphed and pushed harder, driving her arms back and her shoulder blades toward each other. It was actually a pretty pleasant stretch. She sighed. "Some subs will try to resist or trick you to keep the slack in their rope, but most won't lie if you ask them a direct question. Bad manners."

"Now do I get the rope?"

"Look at my arms, first. See how close they are. If they're not that close when the rope is on, then I'm cheating you, and I can probably work myself loose."

She could almost feel the burn of his eyes on her upper back, and she struggled to suppress a shiver. It was...pleasant...to be admired. And she knew he was admiring.

"Go ahead, baby, make me pretty in pink."

"You're already pretty," he murmured, his voice a low tease.

And *then* he finally released her arms. He returned a moment later, trailing a soft, pink cotton rope between her back and her still-clasped arms, until he got to the point above the elbow where she'd taught him to begin the bind. She did shudder this time. She hated being bound, but she loved it, too. She loved everything about ropes, from the way they felt, to the way they flowed through her capable hands as she tied up a willing bottom, to the way they could contain her, biting into her skin and giving her the thing that made her thrill with fear.

"Use your hands to help pull my arms back—don't *just* pull with the rope; that can hurt. That's the way. Now keep it tight. Do you see how I'm flexing my arms? That will give me extra give when I relax them. Watch for it, and don't let your bottoms take advantage—not in a tie like this, anyway. You can encourage her to do it if you want a certain bind to have a little slack." Madame Angelie—ever in control; ever the mistress—kept talking to keep the nerves at bay.

The ropes snaked back and forth across her arms as Tyson made the patient knots she had taught him. And as he worked, she taught him every trick she knew for keeping a tie loose or escaping bondage. Taught him those tricks, and how to circumvent them. By the time he tied the final knot—woven back through the rope and well out of reach of even the most flexible fingers—she was caught and helpless, completely bound. The ropes dug into her arms, taunting her—reminding her—and she closed her eyes and breathed deeply.

"Well done. Do you see the differences from before?" she asked. What she wanted to say was, *Get me the fuck out of this rope.* Her pussy throbbed, hot and heady in response to the adrenaline. *Traitorous bitch.*

"Definitely. So you can't get out?" His voice sounded hesitant, but there was a tinge of excitement underneath.

"No, not on my own."

He stepped closer and ran his fingers up her arms, and she shuddered at the unique sensation of fingers on flesh, skipping over bumps of rope. There was nothing in the world like that stuttered touch, and it was maddening.

"So you're helpless," he mused. She could hear the smile in his voice. Knew he was laughing at her. Knew also that his natural, predatory instincts were not the only things aroused by a helplessly bound woman.

She turned to face him, a teasing grin on her own face, answering his. "You, child, are in a world of trouble when you untie me."

"Maybe I just shouldn't untie you, then," he teased back. He ran his fingers up her waist this time, and she felt just the ghost of his touch through the thick fabric of her corset. He made an approving sound at the wasp waist it gave her. His fingers reached the very top, and he met her eyes with the tips of his fingers just touching the edge of her breasts. He was turned on, but he was respectful, just as she'd taught him.

And damn him, but she was more turned on than she wanted to admit, with the ropes biting into her flesh and adrenaline thrumming through her veins. She gave him the slightest of nods, and he let his fingers continue their wandering, teasing over the raised mounds of her breasts, given volume by the generous boost of the corset. He left gooseflesh in his wake, and smiled at the sight.

"You make one pretty sub," he said. "Pretty in pink."

"But I'm not a sub, and you know it."

"You sure look like one right now," he said. Her hair was up in a casual knot, and he grabbed it, pulling just enough to tip her head back, moving slowly as he bent his lips to her neck, giving her time to stop him.

She sighed as his lips met her soft skin, and let herself swoon into him as her body woke to tingling awareness. His lips made a fiery trail up her jaw, and she gasped and tipped her head back even more, pressing into his hand on the back of her head.

He eased slowly past her jawline, planting one more kiss on her cheek before he lost his nerve, backing away again to see her reaction. Madame Angelie laughed at his expression. "Come on and kiss me, and then untie me."

He swooped in to obey, and she moaned into his mouth as he took her kiss. One of his arms moved around her to play with the ropes up and down her arms, and the unsubtle reminder of her total helplessness poured through her nerves in a shimmer of tingling sparks. He bit down gently on her lip, then thrust his tongue between her teeth, claiming her and overpowering her, just a little.

His other hand dropped lower, tickling at her thigh as he started to explore. "Enough," she said.

Tyson stepped back immediately, touching her only long enough to make sure she was steady on her feet. She turned, and he tugged at the ropes on her arms. Her breath came a little easier as she felt the ropes loosen and slowly fall away.

Free at last, she took a deep, calming breath, and rolled her fingers. When she turned back, Tyson was already coiling the pretty pink cord. She glanced at her arm, enjoying the aesthetics of the rope marks, even as she shivered at the memory of being bound.

"It looks good on you," Tyson said. He lifted a finger and trailed it down one of the marks.

Angelie took his finger and bent it back, putting him on his knees with a moment of leverage. "I let you cage the tiger for a few minutes, my dear, but never forget what kind of a woman you're dealing with in me."

"Okay! Sorry!" She released him and he climbed back to his feet, his body language no longer telling her he was thinking of devouring her.

She smiled. "Have you ever been tied?"

He looked startled. "Of course not."

"Oh?" She quirked one eyebrow at him. "Because no dominant ever lets himself be tied up?"

His eyes went wide as he realized what he'd implied, and he prevaricated, trying to dig himself out of his hole. She held up a hand before he could say anything even more foolish.

"We'll have a private session in a week or so, baby. It's time you learn what it feels like on the *other* side of the ropes. If you want me to keep mentoring you, that is."

Tyson's mouth was open with surprise, but he shut it slowly, considering her, and nodded. "Yes, Madame Angelie."

BUSINESS WEAR

K. Lynn

To most, David Roberts seemed to have it all. He was the vice president of a leading technology company, and lived up to the image of a high-powered executive, right down to his designer suits. But behind the sports cars and fancy dinners, there was the burden of actually running a highly successful company. He was expected to put on a happy face for the public, while behind the scenes he often worked long hours, worried and stressed out over making sure the company maintained its profits each quarter, which was never a guarantee with the fluctuations of the economy lately.

His personal assistant, Steven, was responsible for making sure he showed up where he was supposed to and ate a meal when he had gone too long between snacks, as well as taking care of any menial errands that might distract him from his day. And the young man did it without complaint, even taking the brunt of David's anger when the day was not going so well. Today would qualify as one of those days, and Steven had not escaped David's tirades. His last yelling session took place about an hour before David finally left for the day, but he had not seen Steven since. The entire floor had cleared out long before David had, with only the cleaning crew around to give him a nod of farewell when he emerged from his office.

When he finally made it home to his tenth-floor penthouse, he was still tensed up from the day's issues. One of their suppliers was playing hardball with a competitive offer from a new start-up and David was left to try to smooth it over. They couldn't afford to lose their contract, yet their ten-year history meant nothing when a higher offer was on the table. It had taken David almost the entire day to renegotiate a deal that both sides were fine with, even though Development Designs was left paying more than David had originally wanted to. Because of the unexpected issue, his other appointments got pushed back and he would have to work overtime again tomorrow to make up for it.

David headed through his living room and down the hallway. He was loosening his silk tie as he approached the door, but his hand stilled as he saw the pink Post-it note stuck to the shut bedroom door. It read simply STRIP. His muscles clenched at the implication, but in the back of his mind he felt a sense of relief settling over him as well. He would never relax without some help tonight, and now he had it.

He opened the bedroom door slowly, making sure he was alone for the moment, before going through the motions that were required of him. David had done this before, but he always took great care to not rush. There were rules that he had to abide by, lest the entire session be called off.

Standing beside the bed, he began with his shoes, setting the black leather dress shoes side by side in front of the night-stand and tucking his thin socks into them as well. Next came his red suspenders, unclipped from the waistband of his dark trousers and folded as best as the elastic would allow. He set them down on the floor beside his shoes before starting on his trousers, folding them with care as they became the next item in his growing line of clothing.

With his lower half stripped down to just his tight white briefs, he began on his tie, which was already loosened from his earlier attempts to get comfortable. Once he had removed it from his neck, he took a moment to run his hand down the smooth blue silk. It was imported from Italy, a favored material to complement his wardrobe. David took the time to fold the tie once over, then laid it on the floor as well. Finally came the shirt, white yet no longer crisp after the day's wear. Still, he tried not to put any more wrinkles in it as he folded and placed it on the floor, the last item in the line.

Stripped to skin, and just the thin material of his underwear keeping him from being completely naked, David moved around to the other side of the bed and lay down upon the thin blanket that covered it. The maid had been in earlier, so everything had been put in order, as if waiting for his return. David turned his head so that he was facing the wall, away from the door and his line of clothes, and lay with his palms turned up to the ceiling. The only sound in the room was his stuttered breathing as he awaited his company. He was not allowed to look, not allowed to move or make a sound, until he was told to. He could be waiting only minutes, or laid out in anticipation for half an hour, but any violation of the rules meant the agreement would become invalid and the night's activities wouldn't take place. David couldn't risk that.

It seemed tonight wasn't about long waits, as he heard the bedroom door opening after what seemed like only a few minutes of silence. David kept his head turned, but his ears remained attuned to the room's other occupant. He could tell that his visitor stopped beside the line of David's clothes, bracing a hand on the side of the mattress in order to pick up one of the items. David could wager a guess as to which piece of clothing was chosen, but he wanted to be surprised.

David felt the mattress dip again, this time with the weight of a body slipping onto the bed and crawling across to be near David. His heart quickened as he felt a hand lay upon his right shoulder, and he squeezed his eyes shut with the contact. Then David felt a pressure as the other individual straddled his back. Two hands pressed on each side of David's spine and he could feel the brush of lips against his ear as a masculine voice asked him, "Are you ready?"

He couldn't nod, wasn't allowed to be nonvocal when asked a direct question, so he opened his mouth to respond. "Yes," he paused, his voice cracking over the word, and cleared his throat to try again. "Yes, Sir."

"Good," the man said, then he leaned back so that he was sitting atop David's lower back. "Put your hands above your head."

David did as ordered, stretching his hands up toward the brass rails of the headboard. He felt the pressure release from his back as his companion got off him. David heard the man shuffling as he neared the head of the bed.

"Grab the rails."

He clenched his hands around the thin, cold rails of his headboard. David had bought it when he first moved in, drawn to the intricate detailing of the metal. When his companion saw it for the first time, he mentioned how perfect it was for their purposes. Lying there, his palms pressed against the railings as he awaited his next order, he couldn't help but agree.

"Good to see that you replaced the tie after the accident you had with the last one." David could feel his wrists being bound by the material. "I find the Italian silk to be extra secure, don't you?" His companion pulled tight on the restraints to secure them and David let out an involuntary gasp at the flash of pain it caused.

"Yes, Sir," David managed to say.

The man ran his fingers down over David's arms, over the stretched muscles of his shoulders and back. He paused at David's ass, giving a soft pat to the cotton material before trailing down over his thighs to his ankles.

"No belt today, I see," the man said, pulling at David's right ankle. "But this will be better. More give for you to pull against."

With that, he started wrapping something elastic around David's ankle, pulling the binding back toward the end of the bed. It took David a moment to realize that his suspenders were being used. The elastic material did not weigh against his ankles as his leather belt had in previous sessions, but it did dig into his skin more. And even with the minor flinching he was doing while his companion got him secure, he was already starting to feel the strain. David was likely to have raw marks around his ankles before this was over.

"Are we ready to begin?"

David could feel his heart speed up. He steadied his voice before he chanced a word. "Yes, Sir, I'm ready."

"Good."

He could hear the man moving away from the bed and then there was the sound of wood scraping against wood. David knew what that was, even without looking. His companion had just opened the bottom drawer of the dresser, the one dedicated to these sessions specifically. Inside were a few implements, but they all served the same purpose. He needed release and his companion was going to provide that.

Soon the man was back beside the bed, his left hand laid flat against David's back. "You're tense."

"Yes, Sir."

"And you'd like me to do something about that." It wasn't a question, but he would demand a verbal answer.

"Yes, Sir."

"A massage perhaps?" The man dug his fingers into David's skin, pressing against the tight muscles on each side of his spine.

"No, Sir. I need something else."

"Maybe you need this." And, without giving him a chance to tense up, a pain erupted across David's ass as the flat edge of the paddle came into contact with his underwear-covered buttocks. He didn't have to guess what choice the man had made for tonight; the first hit had confirmed it. The paddle was black leather on one side, able to inflict pain with each swing, but was covered with soft fur on the opposite side to provide some soothing when necessary. It did little when he wasn't fully naked, but it was nice to have the option.

"Did that hurt?" the man asked, rubbing his right hand along David's buttocks. The handle of the paddle trailed over David's sensitive skin as his companion held it and soothed at the same time.

"It felt good, Sir."

"I'm sure it did." The man trailed the soft fur-lined side of the paddle down David's leg until he reached his bound ankles. "Do your bindings feel good, too?"

His companion must have clenched down on some part of the suspenders then because they were suddenly too tight, biting into David's ankles. David arched up, pulling against the headboard, trying to release the rush of pain, but it did little to help.

"What's the matter?" the man asked, landing another blow on David's ass. "Afraid to admit how much you like it?"

"No, Sir," David gasped out, unable to move anywhere without some part of him aching. His ankles would give a little, thanks to the elastic, but then he was pulled back with a firm jolt if he stretched too far. The silk tie had tightened its knot so that it, too, was digging into his skin. Back and forth he went, seesawing between headboard and footboard as the restraints allowed. He tried to flinch away from the paddle by pressing his body deeper into the mattress, but the combined motions had awakened his cock and it was starting to grow firmer with each touch. Pain from the top, pleasure from below, building and growing.

"How much do you need it?" Another blow landed. "Tell me."

"I need it," David said, pressing his body back down to the bed and grinding into the sheets. "Please, Sir, I need it."

"Do you feel trapped?"

David pulled at the tie, but it no longer had any give. "Yes, Sir."

"Just like you feel trapped at work, all day putting up with the stupidities of others, trying to smooth over their mistakes so that the company doesn't suffer." When David didn't respond, another blow came down. "Answer me."

"Yes," David said, his voice shaking. "Yes, Sir."

"And then you take it out on others, cascading down until everyone is as tense as you are." A hand soothed down his back, fingers lightly massaging the tightness there. "But it doesn't help, does it? Nothing helps except this, isn't that right?"

"Yes, Sir."

"Bound here, by me. All the control in my hands." The man braced a hand on David's shoulder and leaned close. "How does it feel to give up all that power, for just a while?"

"Good, Sir." David pulled himself up to get closer to the headboard, in hopes it would relieve some of the strain on his wrists.

"I bet it gets you hot, too," he said, his breath tickling David's ear. "Your cock all hard and ready because of me."

David shifted, his cock becoming more sensitive each time it pressed against the mattress, but it didn't help. He was aching so bad now. "It's ready for you, Sir."

"Arch up," his companion ordered, before moving away.

David tried to comply, pulling his legs so that he could prop up on his knees. The pain around his ankles was relentless, as was that around his wrists. Once he had gotten to his knees, the pressure on his cock was lessened a bit, but not enough. He glanced toward his wrists, the blue silk a striking contrast against the reddened skin around it. There was no blood, but he could tell the rubbing had started to chafe his skin. He would have to wear a long-sleeve shirt tomorrow.

"Looks like you were telling the truth," his companion said, positioning himself behind David so that his own legs were straddling David's. "Let's do something about that."

He began to slip David's underwear down, just enough to release his cock, and let the elastic band snap up snug under David's balls. David flinched at the split second of pain, but then the man's hand was on David's cock and he couldn't think of much else other than pleasure. He looked down and saw the smooth hand encircling his cock, squeezing, and he couldn't suppress a moan. David knew he wasn't going to last long, didn't think his body could hold off even if he wanted to. With each squeeze, he bucked back, his ass coming into contact with his companion. And then he had to push forward again, the pull of the tie around his wrist causing too much pain if he didn't.

On and on they went, repeating the cycle as pain blurred into pleasure and his whole body was tingling.

And then, in one moment, everything stopped; no pain, no pleasure, no sound at all. It was still and then everything went into overdrive as he spilled forth, his cock jerking in his companion's hand and his restraints giving him little room to move. He tried to stay upright, since he had not been given permission to do otherwise, but his legs couldn't withstand the strain. As soon as his companion's hand moved away from his crotch, David fell exhausted to the bed, his face pressed into the mattress and his still-leaking cock staining the sheets beneath. He felt the bed shift as the man moved off, then the sound of the dresser drawer as, he assumed, the paddle was being put away.

David wanted to move, to look and confirm, but instead he just lay resting. Sleep was calling to him and he might have let himself be taken away by it if not for the sudden flash of pain that ran up his arm. His head shot up to look and he saw Steven struggling with the tie, trying to loosen the tight knot it had formed.

"It's not coming loose. I'm going to have to cut it," he said, reaching to open the bedside drawer and remove a pair of scissors. It wasn't the first time David had to be cut out of restraints, but he always mourned the loss of his clothing when it happened.

"Make sure to order me another few to replace this one," David said, letting his body relax back down into the mattress as Steven worked.

Soon his arms were freed, the blood rushing back to his fingers as he laid his hands upon the mattress beside him. They were numb, then tingled as the feeling returned. He saw that his right wrist was encircled with red and the top layer of skin had been worn off during the session. David was sure his left one matched it, but he didn't feel like turning over to check.

His feet were next, but they came loose with much more ease. The elastic of the suspenders had worked out much better than the leather belts they normally used, so he'd have to remember to wear suspenders more often in the future.

David closed his eyes, relaxed and ready to sleep now. He felt the mattress dip on his left, then an arm wrapped around his back to lie against his shoulder.

"Will that be all, Mr. Roberts?" Steven asked, placing a kiss against the back of David's neck.

He thought about answering, but he didn't need to anymore. Instead, he let sleep overtake him. The warm weight of Steven lying beside him was enough to take his mind off anything else.

THE KISSING PARTY

Rachel Kramer Bussel

Who could resist an invitation to a kissing party? Not me. Some people think that kinky people only like the naughty parts of sex, the whips and chains and spankings, the crawling on the floor, the lips pried apart, the nipple clamps, the commands. I love all those things, but I love my husband Derek's beautiful lips more than anything. I could kiss them for hours—and I planned to, when he forwarded me the invitation to the kissing party. Over the years, we've been to our share of swingers clubs, sex parties, and play parties, not to mention the random dinner parties that, after dessert and a few glasses of wine, had turned into mini-orgies, but a kissing party would be something new. From what I could tell, the rules were that you could, and were encouraged to, kiss with abandon, but full-on sexual activity was verboten. How handsy we were allowed to get was up in the air, but I had a feeling we'd find out.

But we are, both of us, kinky to a fault, so he brought a blindfold and, yes, nipple clamps. He put the clamps on me at home, right before I got dressed, lovingly attaching each, then screwing them in. "I'm using these instead of the tweezer clamps so they don't get jostled; it wouldn't be the same if your pretty nipples were set free." So with my nipples trapped between the metal, and our other toys in my purse, we headed off in a cab for Brooklyn, a good half hour ride, with plenty of potholes, along with some jiggling from Derek. By the time we pulled up in front of the bar, I was so wet I almost wanted to go home, or sneak off to an alley where he could give me some relief.

"I thought you wanted to go to a kissing party, Belinda," he teased me, tipping the driver double our fare as he reached his hand down my black wrap dress and gave the man behind the wheel a peek at my nipple. I noticed him smile before Derek pulled me out of the cab.

"I do want to go, baby, but I don't know if I can wear these all night."

"Oh, you can, Belinda, and you will," he said, pulling me close for a kiss that started with my lips slammed hard against his, and ended with him biting my lower lip hard enough to make me whimper. I hurried up the stairs after him as best I could in my towering four-inch black-and-silver heels, my sexiest shoes, ones that conveniently pushed my ass out and my tits forward. Derek paid our entrance fee and ushered me into a lush bar with red-painted walls and erotic art on the walls.

Couples were kissing on bar stools, against doorways, in seats. And not just couples; I saw triple kisses and groupings, foursomes, and one lucky man lay across the laps of three beautiful women, one of whom was leaning down to kiss him. With a hand cupping my ass, Derek led me to the bar. Usually I'd order an extra-dirty martini, but when he ordered me a vodka and cranberry, then turned me around and began to blindfold me, I immediately knew why. I love the elegance of a martini glass, its sleek curves and olive decoration, but trying to drink out of one without seeing what I was holding would surely lead to a martini-soaked dress. Plus Derek likes seeing me put anything in my mouth, mini-straws included.

"And for the lady," the bartender said, making my face warm when I turned back in my seat, knowing the word emblazoned on the blindfold would tell him everything he needed to know about me: SLUT. It was true—for Derek, I was a slut in the very best sense of the word. I'd do anything he asked me to, even if I didn't initially like it, even if it embarrassed me or made me nervous. I love and trust him, and he's never steered me wrong.

"Thank you," I said when Derek pinched my ass, then put my hand out for my drink, but Derek slapped it away.

"Not tonight, my slut." I heard him rummaging around in my bag and seconds later found my wrists being fastened into leather handcuffs behind my back. He must have slipped them in my bag when I wasn't looking. He returned to his stool and said, "Now you can open that pretty mouth," and when I did, he slipped the straw in. It may not seem like such a big deal, sipping a drink from a straw, especially in a room full of people kissing, but when you're wearing a slut blindfold, nipple clamps and handcuffs in public, it becomes a pretty big deal—big enough to make my pussy ache. I took a big sip and then let the straw go.

No sooner were my lips free than Derek was tilting my head toward his and kissing me again. This kiss wasn't like the one we'd shared outdoors. It was soft and slow and tender, his tongue making love to mine, filling me with warmth. I angled closer, tilting my head, taking him in. His hands moved to my cheeks and his tongue took over, invading so I almost couldn't breathe. The kiss finally ended, leaving me trembling. "You have fans, Belinda," he whispered in my ear. "I can see several couples checking you out, admiring how hot you look. I think the friendly thing to do would be to offer to kiss them, don't you?" Of course it wasn't really a question—it never is with Derek. He was telling me that I was about to kiss strangers I couldn't see, under his tutelage.

He gave my cheek a little pat, then a slightly harder one. I moaned, knowing this wasn't the time or place for a full-on slapping session, the kind that leads to him tossing me onto the bed, shoving my ankles up to his hips, and fucking me as hard as he can. Maybe I'd be lucky and get that later. Now it was kissing time.

Derek moved behind me and helped me stand up, keeping an arm around my waist to balance me as I walked in the heels. I heard him say hello to a table of people, then thrust me forward. "This is Belinda. She's mine, but I'm offering her to you to kiss and pet. She likes being used like that, and she's very good with her mouth. Feel free to kiss her here, too," he finished, exposing my clamped nipples, which by then were throbbing.

"Hi, Belinda," cooed a woman's voice. I pictured her with teased bleached-blonde hair and glossy red lips, a modern-day Marilyn Monroe. Her sweet perfume suffused my senses, and soon I was sitting down next to her while her lips met mine. Her lips were sticky with gloss, her tongue tentative at first. I heard murmurings around me but was too focused on the kiss to make out the conversations. The woman's hands brushed the skirt of my dress open enough to expose the fact that I wasn't wearing panties. She left it like that, and kept kissing me, her tongue tickling mine, her gloss smearing into my skin.

Since her hands were tangled in my long brown hair, I knew someone else must have reached for my nipples, thumbs massaging them, rotating each clamped nub. As the touch permeated my body, sending waves of pleasure starting from my nipples and radiating outward, I realized it didn't matter who was touching me. Maybe it was even hotter not to know, not to think, to simply feel. "You can take them off if you want to," I heard Derek say. No one else had ever shared that honor since we'd started dating, and he hadn't told me he planned to allow that. Maybe it was spontaneous. I wasn't sure how I felt about that, but the woman's lips and the mystery hands felt so good, I didn't even think about protesting. Besides, I knew what protesting Derek's plans usually got me, and I wanted to savor the moment.

I tried to prepare myself for the rush of blood about to flood my tender flattened buds, but you can never truly be ready. That's part of the thrill of kink for me—the unexpected, the way even the most familiar activity can catch you off guard, make you feel like a virgin all over again as the pain crashes down.

I felt heady as the woman kissed me deeply, her hands on my cheeks, her perfume invading my senses as my nipples got reacquainted with their freedom. They only had a few moments before someone took one breast in his or her hand and started sucking my nipple. Derek whispered my name in my right ear, a reminder, a warning, a promise. He can make my name sound like the most beautiful aria or the most dreaded epithet, and he knows me well enough to know that in the right circumstances, both of those turn me on.

Then he was kissing the back of my neck, his lips warm, his stubble brushing my skin. I almost laughed at the sensual overload, my dress still splayed open, leaving my pussy on display, while three sets of lips devoured me. Derek's tongue brushed lightly against my neck, a tender contrast to the woman's tongue pressing deep into my mouth and the mouth now sucking deeply on my nipple before biting it just enough to make me gasp.

"Is she being a good slut for you?" Derek asked, loud enough to surely draw the attention of anyone who hadn't already been watching us. "You should see what she looks like with a cock in her mouth and one in her pussy. My girl is happy as long as she has something to fill those pretty lips." No sooner had Derek made that pronouncement than my pussy clenched, making me wonder if I was dripping onto the seat beneath me. The other mouths on me quickly separated from me, leaving my nipple wet and needy, my mouth empty. I rearranged myself as best I could, trapped by the cuffs. I could talk, but what would I ask for? Derek surely knew what I wanted, and I was getting increasingly antsy for him to take me outside and give it to me.

Instead I felt his fingers, four of them, fucking my mouth, making me focus all my energy on stretching around him. He was showing me off, teasing the crowd, making sure they knew exactly how far my oral charms extended. We weren't kissing, but I had a feeling that didn't quite matter by then. We'd already broken a few rules, so perhaps they were ones the crowd had been waiting for to be broken. He kept his fingers in my mouth, but stilled them, so I was left to simply suck and salivate while I listened to the unmistakable sound of him kissing the woman, hearing the same murmurs she'd just made while kissing me. I wondered if he wanted to do more than kiss her, though I would've bet money she wanted to do more than kiss him. I could tell from the noises she was making, the whimpers coming from somewhere deep inside.

"Kiss her again," Derek said, and soon her lips were pressing hard against me. I pictured his hand on her neck, pushing her against me, mashing our mouths together. "It's too bad Belinda has to leave soon so I can make sure she gets fucked good and hard. Maybe I'll have to strap a vibrator inside her next time we attend this party so she can be a little more patient. Give her a hickey as a souvenir," he ordered gruffly, and in seconds the woman's mouth was fastened to my neck, biting hard. I shuddered, surprised he'd let anyone else do that to me.

"Thank you all," Derek said, before he ushered me to my feet and led me away from the table. I'd thought maybe he'd let me see who I'd been kissing, who'd been touching and sucking my nipples, who'd been watching me. Instead he led me to the doorway and only once I felt the promise of the cool air did he undo the cuffs and take off the blindfold. "Kiss me," he commanded, his lips warm, sweet and brutal—just the way I like them.

One newly freed hand found its way to his cock, hard and warm beneath his pants. "I'm not done with you," he told me, as he led me out the door. Now I could see, and hold his hand, but a part of me was still floating, caught up in the high of being on display, being kissed and sucked and used, but only being able to return a fraction of those touches. We quickly reached an alley he seemed to know well, leading me far enough from the street that we couldn't be seen unless someone walked directly past.

"Stand right there," Derek ordered, and lest I expect to keep my mobility, he raised my arms above my head and refastened the cuffs. "Put your arms around my neck." We just fit, him pressed tight against me as he lifted my dress and shoved his fingers inside me. I buried my face in his neck as he fucked me, more ready than I'd realized. In no time I was trembling against him, grateful for the extra support of the wall behind me and his body pressed right up against mine. He kissed me roughly, stealing my breath for a few moments as I came against his fingers, which he quickly withdrew. He undid my arms from his neck and clamped his hand over my mouth as I kept on trembling. I was still so wet and open, and when he let me taste myself on his fingers, I hoped he'd give me his cock next.

But when I'm tied up, when I'm cuffed, when I can't move, Derek likes to make sure I'm fully aware of exactly whose control I'm under. I knew he'd probably love to fuck me right there, pound me into the wall, let my bare ass brush against its coldness, but instead he rearranged me so my bare breasts were hanging out, my dress barely more than a wispy decoration.

With my arms clamped in front of me and my tits hanging between them, he pushed me to my knees, my legs tucked under me, wet slit pressed against my calves. I watched him take out his cock. I immediately stuck out my tongue, hungry to taste him, but even that he wanted to deny me. "I know you wish everyone from the party were here to watch you suck my cock, but they're not. Nobody's here to see what I'm about to do to you." He stroked his cock slowly, teasing me by bringing it so close to my outstretched tongue, letting its dripping head brush once against me before stepping just out of reach. I put my tongue back in my mouth. He hovered over me, aiming his dick right at my tits. It didn't take long before he was groaning, covering my breasts, my cuffs, my fingers and my dress with his come.

He scooped some up and fed it to me, then pulled me up by my joined wrists before unbuckling them. I knew full well he knew I always carry wipes in my purse, but he didn't offer to let me get one out. Instead he took my face gently in one hand and kissed me, while twisting one nipple with the other. He kept kissing me even as he undid the cuffs, tossing them on the ground before returning to greet my lips with his. His sweet, soft kiss combined with his harsh grip, even with his cream coating me, had me aching to touch myself again. With Derek, though, I don't need to be tied up to know when I'm allowed to move. If he wanted me to touch myself, he'd tell me to. Instead I kissed him back until he was done, then covered myself as best I could. He let me put on a sweater and led me to a taxi.

Inside, he smiled at me, recounting our entire evening in a voice loud enough for the driver to overhear. "Maybe we should host our own kissing party," he said as we neared our door.

"Any time," I told him, as I headed up the stairs, his hand on my ass, promising me our night wasn't over yet.

THAT'S NOT A SCRUNCHIE

Giselle Renarde

Did Pella realize the balls it took to ask her out?

It wasn't easy. Didn't matter that they flirted at work every day. Eric felt like he was going to throw up when he invited Pella to dinner and a movie.

Thank god she'd said yes. If she'd turned him down, he would have quit his job, or stabbed himself with a letter opener. It wouldn't just have been humiliating. Eric would have felt…well, heartbroken. Guys weren't supposed to care or whatever, but he wasn't made of stone.

Standing on the wrong side of Pella's door, Eric cupped his hand over his nose and checked his breath. Minty fresh. Perfect. Still, his stomach flipped when he reached up to knock.

Be strong.

He made a fist and rapped at the door.

You never get a second chance to make a first impression.

Eric's heart stopped as he waited for Pella to open the door. He could hear her on the other side, shuffling, jiggling the handle. When the door finally opened, she wasn't there.

"Pella? It's Eric. Where are you?"

"Behind the door," she said without emerging. "Come in for a sec."

"Oh." Eric stepped over the threshold, and the first thing he noticed was a warm scent, like cinnamon and pears. "Okay, thanks."

Pella's apartment was really dark inside. Even when she'd closed the door behind him, Eric strained to find her shape in the shadows.

"Take off your shoes?" she asked. "I just got new area rugs."

"Oh yeah, you were saying." Eric scuttled out of his shoes without untying the laces. "From the Persian shop on Yorkville, right? Those places scare the crap out of me."

"Persian places?"

"No, no, I meant *boutiques*." His heart raced. Pella must know by now that he didn't have anything against her culture or ethnicity, whatever you call it. "Fancy stores freak me out, you know? I always feel like they're gonna give me the bum's rush because they don't like my pants."

"Your pants?"

Pella took a step forward, and Eric took a step back. As she forced him into the candlelit living room, he got his first look at what she had on: black silk, with ribbons crisscrossing her front. Very short. *Very* short. It wasn't a dress, was it? It wasn't something you'd wear out of the house.

"Oh, you're not...ready?" Eric swallowed hard.

"I'm ready," she said, almost a growl.

He knew he was staring at her cleavage, but he couldn't help himself. Pella never dressed like this for work—low cut, silky, seductive. Her legs were completely bare, from her thighs down to...actually, she did have shoes on, with little heels and black straps. Her toenails were painted with dark polish. Purple, maybe? Hard to tell in the candlelight.

"You're ready...to...go out?"

Pella threw her head back and laughed. Rather than answer, she pressed him across the room, unzipping his pants and letting them fall down his legs. What the hell was she doing? Taking off his underwear? Was this really happening, or had he hit his head on the way over?

In the darkness, Eric had no idea where he was stepping. He wasn't entirely surprised when he fell on a couch. Really, the fact that he was naked from the waist down was more of a shock.

"We're here!" Pella cooed. "Happy first date."

"I thought we were going out," he said. "Dinner and a movie."

"Everybody does dinner and a movie." Pella fell to her knees and grabbed hold of a silky black cord. "I thought we might start our evening off with a little light bondage."

Eric's cock surged as he realized what was going on. She'd planned this, obviously. Pella always was the most organized person in the office, but Eric had never known anyone to be so prepared in the bedroom. Not that they were in her bedroom. No, Pella obviously wanted him on the couch—she'd tied ropes to the heavy wooden feet, and was now in the process of securing those ropes to his ankles. He let her, of course. He was really too shocked to move.

"Put your arms out," Pella instructed. She didn't wait for him to move before grabbing his wrists and stretching them out across the back of the sofa. "Very good. You've done this before."

"I'm pretty sure I haven't," Eric said, chuckling with nerves.

Pella had obviously tied two cords to the back legs of the

couch, because now she was tying his wrists up, too.

"You've never been bound like this?" She knotted the rope tightly.

"Not to a couch. Not on a first date." *Not at all*, but he didn't want to seem like a bondage virgin when Pella was obviously so keen on it.

"How does that feel?" she asked. "Too loose? Too tight?"

"Definitely not too loose." The ropes splayed him like a butterfly, so wide his inner thighs burned. He was open to her, open for her, and it hit him how vulnerable he was. "What were you planning, exactly?"

Pella cocked her head and smiled. "Nervous?"

His cock jumped, drawing her gaze. "Should I be?"

Shuffling between his open thighs, she shrugged. "That depends, I suppose."

"Depends on what?"

She leaned her naked knees against the front of the couch and unbuttoned Eric's stiff shirt, slowly, top to bottom. The pace was torture. What was she planning? He had a few ideas of what might be in store, but Pella worked in mysterious ways.

"Ahh, look at your chest!" She wove her fingers together beneath her chin, smiling rapturously. "My god, you're fit. I thought you'd look good, but this... this is a nice surprise."

Eric's cock waved with delight, and Pella chuckled sweetly. He wanted to return the compliment, but what could he say? *You look good? You look great?* Everything sounded stupid, in his mind. With all his blood flowing straight to his crotch, he couldn't form a proper sentence.

"You look...wow..."

Well, it was better than nothing.

"*Wow*, do I?" Pella fell between his legs, slowly stroking his thighs. "I look *wow*..."

"Sorry," he said. "My brain is not…working."

She grinned and angled her fingers, so the nails caught his skin. She traced them slowly down his thighs, digging just deep enough to make him writhe against his bindings.

"No, I like it. *Wow*. I take that as a compliment."

"It was definitely intended that way," he told her as she traced her nails up his thighs.

His cock lurched at her hand, but she swept it out of the way, teasingly. It landed like felled lumber, splashing precum down his leg. He didn't want to let her see how fucking good that felt, but how could he possibly hide it? She'd got him colossally aroused, tying him up spread-eagle across the couch, then tracing those vicious fingernails across his flesh.

Now she was kneeling between his legs, waiting.

He admired her control and precision. She had this all planned out in her mind, didn't she? Pella knew just what she wanted.

She traced the backs of her fingernails up his thighs, and beyond—up the ridges of his belly, up his chest. When she wrapped her fingers around his neck, the sparkle in her eyes tied Eric's stomach in knots. What was she doing? She wouldn't strangle him. No, she couldn't. Even bound up, he could certainly escape. Couldn't he?

Pella giggled as she ran her hands down his chest. "You're cute when you're scared."

"Am I?" Eric didn't want to feel shaken, but this was all new to him. "Thanks."

"What about me?" she asked, planting kisses down the tight, arching muscles of his belly. "Am I cute?"

"Cute, yes. Scared? Doesn't look like it."

Her lip twitched before a smile took over. "Right…"

Eric gazed down at the girl hovering over his hard cock. Pella, from the office. Pella, his work friend. His reason for getting up in the morning—not that he'd ever told her that. As his erection whacked her magnificent cleavage, it occurred to him that she was every bit as apprehensive as he was. She was just better at concealing her fear.

Swallowing hard, Eric raised his hips off the couch, driving his cock into the tight valley between Pella's breasts. He was just riding the surface, but even the slightest touch brought amazement through his body, from his dick, right up through to his heart. He'd never felt anything so intense.

"Look at this cock," Pella said in a whisper.

She bowed her head and spit.

As soon as that wet warmth met his red-hot tip, she pressed her thumb against it, rubbing her spit and his precum all over his cockhead. Her hands were everywhere! One clenched tight to the top of his shaft, moving only slightly while the other hand found his balls.

"Oh, for fuck's sake!" Eric threw his head back, but it snapped up again. "What are you doing to me?"

Bending forward, Pella brought her breasts out through the low V-neck of her black silk. Eric's breath hitched as her exposed nipples met the cool evening air. They tightened into dark, pebbled buds. In the candlelight, her flesh glowed like bronze.

Setting her big breasts on Eric's thighs, Pella bowed her head and spit on his dick. Who'd have thought it could feel so good? But, then, who'd have thought a first date would turn into... this?

As Pella bent forward, something slipped down her head, falling to the floor, and releasing a waterfall of hair over her perfect shoulders.

"Your scrunchie," Eric said, nodding to the floor. "It fell out. It's right there."

"My scrunchie?" Pella appeared amused. She picked up the black elastic and asked, "This? It's not a scrunchie."

"Oh."

"It's a hair band."

"Oh." Eric gazed from her luscious breasts to the elastic in her hand. "Well, what's a scrunchie?"

Who cares? Why was he asking stupid questions?

Pella bit her bottom lip, like she was looking up the definition in her mind. "A scrunchie is one of those big hair ties they wore around ponytails in the eighties. The ones with fabric around them. This is not a scrunchie, it's just an elastic you put around your head to keep hair out of your face."

"Oh." This had to be the longest conversation Eric had ever had about hair products. "Okay."

"It's good for other things, too," Pella said, weaving the long elastic around her fingers. She suddenly seemed more interested in the elastic than she was in Eric. He wasn't sure exactly what to do about that.

But his cock wasn't so subtle. It leapt forward to whack Pella's tits, spilling precum across the expanse of her flesh.

"Somebody's eager," she said with a laugh.

"Looks like."

Pella's expression darkened as she took his balls in hand. She gripped them tight, making them strain against his sac. Eric was so shocked he didn't make a sound. He didn't even struggle and she wound her hair elastic around his balls. At first, it didn't really register what she was up to. She'd already tied up his wrists and his ankles. Now she was tying up his balls?

The strain was like nothing he'd ever felt before. It was painful, but it didn't hurt. He felt strung up and weak, but the harder his cock strained, the stronger he felt, too. Nothing made sense.

"How's that?" she asked, though she seemed to know already.

"Good." What else could he say? How was it supposed to feel?

"Ready for more?"

"I don't know..."

She smirked as she wrapped her full breasts around his dick. God, they were warm. Warm and wonderful. His balls strained against the underside of her boobs as she began moving them, just slowly, at first. Slowly gobbling up his entire dick with her full, fleshy breasts.

"You like that?" She spit again, and it landed deep inside her cleavage. He could feel it against his throbbing shaft.

"How could you tell?"

As her cleavage consumed his cock, Eric tightened his asscheeks without really meaning to. It was the only way he could thrust. Every time he squeezed his butt, he felt it through his balls. That bound-up pair clenched tight, driving a strange pleasure through his shaft. He felt huge inside the cavern of Pella's cleavage.

"God, Pella." Eric's breath rattled in his lungs. "What are you doing to me?"

She pinched her nipples, and he could have sworn he could feel it, too. When she bit her bottom lip, his balls quaked. They were trying to creep up close to his body, he realized, but the band kept them at bay. All he could do was sit there and watch as she fucked him with her tits, riding him hard and hot. How was she doing that? And was she enjoying it as much as she seemed to be?

Eric bucked between Pella's beautiful tits. Hard to believe this was the very first interaction he was having with them. Usually, the sequence went: look, touch, suck, nibble. Fucking might not happen at all, and certainly not on a first date.

"You're killing me," Eric moaned as Pella curled her head down to lick his cockhead. "Oh, for fuck's sake!"

She giggled deep in her throat. Her hair tumbled forward, dancing down the sides of his bare thighs. Jiggling her tits on his erection, she sucked just the tip between her full, luscious lips.

"Christ, I'm gonna come if you keep doing that."

She made a noise that sounded like "Good" without even opening her mouth. Eric's body didn't feel like his own. It moved of its own volition, bucking against his bindings, throbbing against that not-a-scrunchie.

"Don't you want..." How could he phrase this without sounding full of himself? "I mean, you don't want to...?"

To fuck me? You don't want to pull up that little silk number and sit on my hot fucking dick?

Pella moaned around his cockhead, sucking just that most sensitive bit while her tits wrapped around him like a tight pussy. Everything about her struck him as elegant—even the way she bounced on his hard-on. It was more like writhing, like an undulating mass of flesh. God, he loved her curves. What a body! What a great fuck!

Every suck brought him to the brink, but nothing put him over. It must have been the elastic, compressing his balls, keeping his cum from coming out. Without it, he'd have exploded forty times over by now.

"Can you take off the scrunchie?"

Pella mumbled something around his cock, but he didn't understand.

"I want to come, please!" Eric clenched his ass and bucked off the couch, getting so close to orgasm he could almost taste it. "Fuck, you gotta take off the scrunchie!"

Pella jerked up and his cockhead popped out of her mouth. "It's not a scrunchie!"

Her eyes blazed. Eric got the same feeling he'd had when he thought she was going to strangle him. Then a grin broke across her lips, and Eric rolled his eyes. "Fine, then can you take off the *elastic*?"

With a full, toothy smile, Pella said, "Sure."

She didn't even unwrap her breasts from around his cock before digging underneath to fondle his balls.

"Oh, that's good." Eric bucked against her breasts, but they weren't so tight now that her hands were otherwise engaged. "No, you know what? Leave it."

"Leave it?" Pella wrapped her hands around her huge breasts and hugged them around his begging cock.

He wasn't sure what she'd done, exactly, but the elastic around his balls felt a little looser. He tested the waters, fucking her tits slowly. Her lips parted gently, and stayed that way, like she was gasping silently. She seemed worlds away, transported by pleasure. Did this really feel as good for her as it did for him?

Eric planted his feet firmly on the floor. Harnessing all the strength left in his legs, he drove his erection between Pella's breasts, so hard his balls lodged themselves somewhere inside her cleavage.

Pella growled like a bear in heat as she plunged her face against her boobs, swallowing as much of Eric's cock as was sticking up between them. How could she bend that way? How could anyone be so flexible?

She hugged her breasts, squeezing his balls and the root of his cock. Christ, how was she doing that? The pressure was immense. She squeezed him tight, like she was trying to squeeze the cum right out of him...

And, fuck, it was working!

Pella mewed and squealed as she sucked his cockhead. Eric's

balls pulled up tight to his body—as tight as they could get, considering they were bound up—and Pella pulled away just as he released his first gusher.

"Yessss!" she hissed as white cream splattered across her tits. "Oh god, look at that hot jizz!"

So dirty!

Eric shot another load when those smutty words registered. Pella threw her head back and shuddered. Her breasts jiggled around his dick, drawing out more cum. She might as well have been sucking it through a straw!

Letting go of her breasts, Pella dug her fingernails into Eric's thighs and arched back. Yet more cum spilled across her chest, painting white over bronze like a Jackson Pollock canvas.

Beautiful.

Pella fell back on her heels, dragging her nails the length of his thighs. His cock strained for her, but he was spent. Totally spent. He ached to get hard again, so she could unleash him and wrap her wet pussy around his dick, but that wasn't going to happen. He was gone, exhausted. He could have slept right there, tied to the couch. Easily.

"That was..." Pella shook her head, completely out of breath. "Wow!"

"See? I told you *wow* was a compliment." Eric chuckled, shuffling against the couch. "Do you think you could take off this...scrunchie?"

She smirked, then smacked his thigh. "It's not a scrunchie."

"I know. Just teasing."

When she peeled off the elastic, her touch made him laugh. It tickled. She didn't seem to realize how sensitive his flesh was.

Or maybe she did. Hard to tell...

"We'll probably miss our dinner reservation, but the movie's not until nine." Eric watched keenly as Pella stood between his legs. "Did you still want to go out?"

"I don't know." Pulling off her silk chemise, she stood naked before his bound-up body. "Whatever you like."

VALLES MARINERIS

Laila Blake

She has a thing about Mars, my baby girl.

Kneeling at my feet in her cozy one-room apartment, she has her cheek on my thigh, reading the official NASA blog on her iPad. Her fingers glide over the screen like a dance. She is an involved reader—never completely silent. Sometimes, she huffs or snorts; she utters those tiny little pleasure sounds when she smiles or hums in agreement—it's the cutest thing. I have my hand on the back of her neck where I can just feel the warm leather collar she put on before meeting me at the door. I caress her scalp, get distracted from the essays I brought with me to grade. Her hair smells like flowers, soft and with that hint of dampness from when she showered earlier. Everything about her is supple, from her heart-shaped face to her breasts, her stomach, her rounded thighs. Kneeling there, she is all velvety warm curves and skin, shaved and moisturized. Naked of course, but that goes without saying.

I like her apartment. Mine of course has the collection of

implements and toys, the benefit of my home ground—but coming here is like stepping into her head, into her personality. Around her bed, the entire corner—both walls and ceiling—are covered in a huge red mural of the planet Mars, intricate and well rendered with its craters and valleys. She has so many books all over the room but I've never seen her touch any of them— she always reads on her iPad. Over her desk is a large framed picture of the blue police box in "Doctor Who" and secretly, I am sure that she chose the sofa color because it matched the Tardis so well.

She is not one of my students—that's important to me. I teach college freshmen and sophomore sociology. She's waiting tables, tutoring, writing articles for science magazines—waiting to hear about her PhD proposals. Chemistry.

I must have seemed distracted because she looks up at me with her huge hazel eyes and bites her lip.

"Do you want me to put the computer away?" she asks. I smile, have a look at the stack of mediocre essays that hasn't shrunk in the last hour and finally nod. She finds the OFF button and slides the tablet onto the coffee table. Then she smiles up at me again. I don't know if it is instinct or by design but she pushes her breasts out as she leans back to regard my face. Hers is upside down and I pet her cheek, her nose; I let my fingers enter her willing mouth.

"Suckle..." I whisper and she obeys. Her tongue swirls around my finger before her lips close tightly around my knuckle. Warm wetness engulfs my finger and she sucks it in to the hilt. I brush along the very back of her tongue and up toward her soft palate until she gags a little. I love making her gag, that tiny choking sound that goes with a jerk through her entire body, every muscle jumping to attention with just a tiny stroke of my finger. Even her eyes widen, glisten with that reflex to water.

When I take it slow, I can push my finger all the way into her throat, can feel her muscles contract and spasm around it. My cock aches for her.

"Such a good little pet," I whisper, and she sucks harder. Her eyes close in lustful concentration—with that adorable little wrinkle between her brows. She has the same expression on her face when she does complicated formulas, which doesn't sound like a compliment, but it is on her beautiful little face.

I insert a second finger, then a third. She can't close her lips around them tightly anymore and saliva drips down her chin. Messy little pet. The slurping noises, wet and sticky, are delightfully suggestive; she gags again and it makes her breasts shake a little longer than the rest of her body. I yearn to spank them pink and make them dance.

I let my free hand trail down her neck and find one of her nipples. They are small, cute pebbles on her weighty breasts— good for squeezing. Fucking her mouth with my fingers, I lift her breast up by that nipple. She groans; her body is trapped in that moment where her impulses tell her to try to free herself but her desires lock her in place. She wriggles, shakes, her eyes are watering but heat radiates from her body and I can see her trying to push her cunt onto her heel for pressure.

My eyes are caught by her mural again. It draws you in, like a spell. When I first stepped into her apartment—I was taking her out on our second date—I made the mistake of commenting.

"And here I thought women are from Venus," I said. Even then, I didn't truly think it funny, just something you said to break the ice. I cringed at the look on her face, though—the first time, I thought she might not pick up the phone anymore when I'd call her the next day. She seemed to decide to ignore it though, picked up her jacket and changed the subject.

"Venus is poisonous." It was later at dinner at the small Thai place I'd taken her to that she picked the topic up again, calm and with a sweet smile on her face. "They named it for the goddess of beauty because it's the brightest object in the night sky...apart from the moon of course. They thought it so stunning. Now we know that we can't even see its surface because the entire planet is surrounded by clouds of sulfuric acid and an atmosphere of carbon monoxide." Her voice tends to lower when she talks about the universe, her eyes grow intense and she leans forward. That day, she blushed a little, as though afraid I might find her less attractive for her passions and yet unable to stop. "Venus is like...one of those mean girls in high school. Beautiful from afar, but... you don't want to get too close. She'll burn anyone who does."

"And Mars?" I asked, wanting her to continue, wanting to see more of those intricate changes her face went through.

"Mars...doesn't pretend to be anything it isn't," she said quietly, blinking and reaching for her apple juice. "No atmosphere, no clouds. It's open; doesn't have any protective shields. Mars is scarred, it's most likely the remains of some ancient catastrophe—but it's still there, still beautiful, showing its scars to the world."

I fucked her that night for the first time under that Mars mural. I tied her hands to her bedposts and choked her as she came...twice. Then she curled up in my arms and fell asleep there. For almost an hour she made the softest little pleasure sounds with every exhale—as though her body was still in afterglow. I wanted to hold her safe forever.

"Get on the bed," I say. My voice is hoarse with desire; there's decidedly too little space in my pants. "Hands and knees, face on the blanket, pet."

When I take my fingers from her mouth, they are sticky with saliva. For a heartbeat, a transparent string spans the distance between her lips and my hand before it snaps. She is breathing hard but smiling.

"Yes, Sir," she whispers—hoarse and whimpering—and immediately turns around to crawl across the room. She must be feeling the carpet burn but she doesn't show it; her ass sways and her open cunt is glistening in excited expectation. I don't move from my spot until she climbs onto the bed and situates herself there, cheek pressed into the sunset-colored sheets. The fairy lights she's slung around the headboard throw interesting light effects on her skin. If you believe fashion magazines and those popular TV shows she watches sometimes, she could stand to lose some pounds—but that just goes to show that they have never seen a woman like this, kneeling on that bed, her beautiful round ass high in the air, folded over into a cute little package of herself—warm and soft and inviting. I watch her for a while, how she tries to stay motionless but how her ass sways anyway, wriggles from time to time to try to compensate for the mounting arousal.

When I push myself off the couch, I take a deep breath and rearrange my pants. Space feels good but so did the rising pressure.

My hand is still wet with her saliva. I use the other to pull her asscheeks apart and spread it down her crack.

"Good shave, pet," I whisper, and she whines in response. My fingers glide down over her sphincter; it contracts like a shy flower. Her ass shakes when I smack it. Her whole aura is filled with the beautiful bouquet of cunt and flowery moisturizer and I step inside of it like stepping into an alluring bubble.

I let my fingers roam down to her cunt, too. So wet and sweet, then drag her juices up to her ass again. She wriggles and whines—the massive scar on her back glitters in the fairy lights. The scar tissue is darker than the rest of her skin, its edges ragged like the fjords of Norway. Its texture is glossier, seems thinner and more fragile. It took her a while to let me see her like this—her scar on display. It was a chemical burn she said, but when I pressed her for details, she kissed my neck and her fingers slipped to my crotch to encircle my cock. She has beautiful hands.

I push her hair from her back to see it in its full spread—crossing her back from her right shoulder over her spine and fading out at her left hip. She sometimes talks about finding a way to get a tattoo artist to turn it into something beautiful—but it already is. I can see her look back at me nervously; I smile and run my fingers down the frayed edges while the other starts to encircle her clit. She is breathing more heavily now, her face is flushed.

In the small of her back, just over the dimples she has there, my fingers find the familiar circular burns. Three, in a neat row. Cigarette burns, clearly. I didn't do that to her, someone before me did. I always find it both painful and exhilarating to find these marks of her sexual history on the very skin I love to kiss.

"Tharsis region," she whispers, voice soaked in need.

"Mmm?"

"That's what they are," she says, and swallows, pushing her ass back against my hand little a kitten looking for more petting. "The three volcanoes of the Tharsis bulge. On Mars." She makes a vague nod up at the mural. "Valles Marineris and the Tharsis bulge. I asked for them."

"Did it hurt?" Fascinated, I can't stop sliding my fingers over the shiny white burns. She nods and I lean over to kiss each of them in turn. Somehow, my other fingers have made it into her cunt and I am pumping it harder now. I don't ever want to hurt her like that and still, I feel jealous. I imagine the smoke of the cigarette, the smell of charred flesh—it should turn my stomach but it doesn't; it makes my cock so hard it hurts.

"Did you cry?" Again she nods; I can actually see the tremor run down her spine and I pull my fingers from her cunt.

"I'm going to fuck you..." I exhale, my voice is shaky—I hate when that happens, or when I get so desperate to have her, my hands can't get the button to open immediately. "Beg me, ask me to fuck your ass, pet."

"Please, Sir," she obliges immediately, "please, please fuck my ass, please?" She used to find this so difficult but it slips easily over her tongue now, needy and honest. She wriggles again, and I run my fingers over the tight ring of muscle. I want her so much, my head hurts and before she can guess what I am about to do, I push my cock deep into sopping cunt. She cries out loud and I push in hard and deep, once and then again. Both my hands find purchase on her asscheeks and I pull them apart. Again, she cries out and I wonder if I was too rough, but then she whimpers and moans for more.

"Please, Sir...pleeeaaase...?"

Words that could squeeze my heart bloody every time.

I pull out and find her ass. My cock is slick with her juices but nothing else. I don't want to prepare her today. Not today. Instead I rub the head of my cock over crack, back and forth, back and forth. I aim a gob of spit right at the top, where her round cheeks form that delicious fold and then smear it all over. She can't stop shaking, whimpering, pleading with me.

When I push past that ring of muscles, she fists the sheets. Her moan is almost inhuman—I realize I want her to cry, just like that time she asked some ex to burn those Tharsis volcanoes into the small of her back. I push it in to the hilt and then pause. I hear her sniffing but she looks back at me and her eyes are glowing. She is so tight. I have to exhale a shaky sigh, too. It almost hurts it's so good.

"Please...Sir?" she gasps and I want to kiss her and hold her forever. Instead, for the moment at least, I fuck her.

I take hold of her hair for leverage, and I fuck her hard and long, pull up her torso so that I can bite her shoulder when I cum.

We slump over to the side; her ass contracts a little around my slowly softening cock. She exhales a moan with each breath and I kiss the Valles Marineris carved down her back. My pet, my beautiful baby girl—she has a thing for Mars.

WHAT
SHE HAS

Sommer Marsden

"You want what she has." Carl's voice is up close. His breath washing across my face. He smells like the mints he keeps in his pocket since he quit smoking. His lips drag along the slope of my shoulder, provoking the need to shiver.

I repress it.

"I saw you looking at it. All night long. Your focus should have been on me. On our dinner and our visit with Peter and Callie and yet, all your focus was on her."

It's true. I chew my lip and wait. My heart is knocking so hard I feel heat flood my body. A hot flash spurred by panic. My wrists trapped in soft leather cuffs are clipped together so I have no play. I try to loop my joined arms over my raised knees and curl in on myself. Carl stops me.

"I don't think so." He pushes my legs flat so I'm sitting up straight and proper, bound wrists in my lap, eyes blindfolded so I have no fucking clue what he's going to do. I can't even tell how angry he is because he always keeps his voice calm and even. It's his face, his dark green eyes, that let me read the tide of his emotions.

"Tell me I'm wrong, Edie," he says.

I shake my head and swallow hard. My stomach cramps with worry. He's not wrong. He's absolutely right. All I could focus on was that fucking new collar on Callie's trim neck. Supple black leather, thinner than most, but thick enough to fit a small D-ring. She'd cocked her head and moved her shoulders and done everything but point to it to show the thing off. I had wanted to just be happy for her. The physical proof of her bond with her master. Instead, I just felt jealous.

What Carl and I have is better. I am better. I'm a better sub, a better girl, a better...everything. She is usually bitchy and bratty and it isn't to prompt a punishment if she's in the mood. It's just because she is a brat.

My throat is thick with emotion and shame.

Something taps my haunch. A flap of leather. A crop. My heart picks up again.

"I asked you to speak, Edie. I'm confused as to why you haven't spoken."

"You're not," I blurt. "Not wrong. I was...I *am* jealous." I blow out a breath and straighten my spine as if to say: *There. Are you happy?*

Carl chuckles. That could be good. That could be bad.

"Where should your focus have been tonight, Edie?"

I blush. I know the answer. I always know the answer. It's a no brainer. And yet, it clearly isn't what I did. I'd behaved terribly. I know this. "My focus should be on you."

The leather flap of the crop slides up my calf, tickles under my knee, moves high to caress my trembling thigh. I feel goose bumps rush to life under the sensation. My heart does a restless little flip, but between my thighs I'm all wetness and heat.

"And was your focus on me?"

He strokes the crop over my belly, carefully inserting it between the inverted *V* of my arms since I don't feel it at all until it's licking at my skin. He drags it a bit lower and the leather prods my mound. I'm nude and cold and blind and...waiting.

"No, Sir. It was not."

"Where was it?"

There is a fleeting slip of leather between my legs. My clit thumps at the brief contact and then hums needily with blood. But there is no more sensation. No more touch there. Of course not, I'm being reprimanded.

"On Callie. On her collar."

"You're not even a leather girl," he laughs.

I frown. I feel my face turn down—quite unattractive, but his amusement hurts me some. Part of my heart seems to crimp up in an almost painful way.

"I know, Sir."

I'm not. I don't prefer leather. I prefer prettier things. My leather cuffs are cobalt blue because it's my favorite color and he spoils me. The crops and whips and paddles are all his. They are manly—black and sleek and mostly leather. But the stuff that will be on me is always prettier; he likes to please me. For heaven's sake, the butt plug he likes best is pink glass. Pink because I thought it was pretty.

"Then what was the problem?"

I shrug. Too embarrassed to say.

"Come now." The crop nudges just beneath my chin, lifting my face up toward him even though I can't see him.

All I can focus on is the wet thrumming between my legs and the embarrassed heat in my cheeks.

"Edie..." There's warning in his voice.

I shake my head. Press my lips together.

"Turn over then," he says.

I hold my hands out, try to obey, but my balance is off and my body has taken up a fine tremor from a bizarre combination of shame, anxiety and excitement. I always feel topsy-turvy when he punishes me. Sometimes he punishes me because I've disobeyed. Sometimes because we both need it. Sometimes as just a prelude to a good fuck. There are all kinds of layers to punishment. What has me nerve-racked and antsy is that I can't read this one.

Is he amused? Is he flabbergasted? Disappointed? Angry? Does he understand my feelings or does he think me petty? If I could see him...

He hardly every blindfolds me for this long. He prefers to watch the emotion in my eyes. So maybe this is it, he's really truly angry with me.

His big hands are on me, helping me move to my belly. "Hands beneath you," he says almost clinically as if he's the physician and I'm the patient. He's here to cure me of my jealousy, I think wildly.

My hands nestle beneath my pelvis, the discomfort reminding me this is not just him playing with me. This punishment will be for a very real transgression. I had behaved like a petty child and the worst of all was that Callie had known how I felt. She'd eaten it up. That bitch.

"Stop reliving it," he says, smoothing a hand down my back. "Your whole body is rigid, Edie. Let it go."

I blow out a long breath, tears pricking my eyes even as my skin responds greedily to his firm but gentle touch. The fact that he knows me so well—is pretty much in my head—is both comforting and unnerving.

"Don't you know it's wrong to covet?" Something different slides up the back of my calf, traveling up my thigh to brush along my asscheeks, and then it disappears. The sensation of it cool, almost cold, and unyielding. But then the crop is back and my pulse jacks up.

Crops are my least favorite. They are somewhat impersonal. Paddles do fine by me. They're almost as terribly pleasant as a bare-handed spanking. Whips I favor because he only gives me a few good licks before he worries about my "pretty skin" and by then he's so frothed up he's usually bending me over something. Taking me...

My cunt flexes eagerly around nothing at all. My stomach is light with anticipation. My ears hissing with white noise prompted by my pounding pulse.

The crop settles along the bottom swell of my buttocks and he says, "I'd like you to say, 'I will not covet Callie's tokens for every stroke.' Do you understand, Edie?"

I forget myself and nod. No noise from him. Not a bit. Nothing but the tick of the clock and the sound of a car horn out in the real world. Far away but still audible.

"Yes, Sir," I cover quickly.

"Good girl."

I can't help it. My chest puffs up with pride when he says that. Doesn't matter that my breasts are crushed to the bedding and my shoulders are starting to sing from restriction and my pussy is wet and ready but empty. All that matters in that moment are those two words.

The first lick of the crop is sharp and fast. Like a razor blade slicing skin before you even know it's there. It's a sharp incision-like sensation and then it's gone.

"I will not covet Callie's tokens," I gasp. I want to cry but I swallow it down. I deserve this.

He slides the tip of the crop down the crack of my ass, stimulating that bundle of nerves right at my tailbone that always makes me have to pee. That sudden yet fleeting urge makes me writhe even more beneath him. Before I can focus my mind and steady my breath, the crop drags a line of fire along my opposite asscheek.

"I will not covet Callie's tokens," I cry. "And I was worried Peter loved her more than you love me!" I blurt it, finally answering his question. I'm ashamed of what I've just said.

I mean it. What the fuck am I thinking? What I have with Carl is so far beyond what she has with Paul. But then I shake my head, realizing that is not the point. I shouldn't compare.

"Never. He could never love her more," he says calmly. And then: "You're saying the words but you don't quite believe them. Coveting what others have and forgetting to cherish what you have is a bad way to go," he says. The leather tip of the crop drags along my spine and then he lays three sharp blows along the very tops of my thighs. It's like being branded three times in quick succession and my body arches up, humping over my own hands, from the blows.

I cry out in frustration and pain and then he gives me a moment to feel that sudden rush of discomfort pooling into a thick warming pleasure. My pussy is pounding in time with my heart. All I want in the world is for him to fuck me. To make it better. But first I deliver three gasping recitations of my commitment to not covet Callie's trinkets.

"How many was that?" he asks.

I go blank. Panic fills me and then I let my body tell me. I focus on each hot line of discomfort currently keeping time with my pulse. "Five."

"Good girl. And how many years have we been together now?"

"Six," I answer, dutifully.

"And what's my favorite number?"

I can't help but smile. "Six," I say.

"Good. So, let's pretend we're in math class. We've done five and my favorite number is six. How many blows do we have left to go, Edie?"

"One," I answer, my voice muffled by the plump pillows beneath my head.

"Wrong!" He says it almost gleefully as I wriggle under his gaze. I can't see him but I swear I can *feel* him studying me. He's memorizing his handiwork. The pattern that his crop has left on the pale smooth skin on my backside.

"I...um, Sir?"

"Two," he says, his lips brushing my earlobe. He's leaned over me. I can feel his heat and his presence. It seems huge and dwarfing with my eyes covered.

I jump with surprise as he begins to lay gentle kisses down my spine. His lips find the small of my back, and he drags his tongue lower. More kisses, provoking little jerks of my body, over the warmed skin of my ass where he's left his disciplinary mark.

"You should not worry about what she has," he says to me, his tongue flicking along my asscrack, dragging just beneath my ass where thigh meets bottom. "You should focus on what you have."

I know he's right but I can't say a word because my brain has shut down. My body is responding quite violently to his ministrations and I grind my hips against my clasped, trapped hands, hoping to get some friction. I'm so desperate for some contact between my legs. I'm so desperate to get off.

"Don't you dare," he says, biting my bottom none too gently.

I jump and immediately still my wayward hips.

"Now for those two strokes," he says. And then there is just silence. Nothing but. I wait and I wait, ears straining to pick up any sound of him. I'm almost certain he's gone from the room when the first blow falls right across the backs of both thighs. My back arches and my mouth presses down into a tight seam. Another blow and I let the sob I've been holding on to fly off my lips. Because that is it. Two. He said two and that was two.

Now he'll take off the blindfold and—

But he doesn't. The bed dips with his weight, and he yanks me up on my knees. He knocks my legs wider with his knee, and I hear his zipper hiss. The perfunctory nature of it has me panting, desperate for him. His cock drags from my slick opening all the way back to tease at, but not breach, my ass. Then he slides back to my waiting cunt and pushes in just enough for me to feel him there. I want to drive myself back, fill myself with him, but know that pushing him would probably result in no fucking at all.

"I was disappointed in you," he says, sliding in another inch.

I bite my tongue to keep from begging. To keep from crying out. I feel like I might scream.

"But then…" His hand strokes my lower back. "I was disappointed in me. I think maybe you don't understand what you mean to me…"

"No," I say, tossing my head. "That's not—"

"Hush."

I hush. He slides in another inch and stills again. I want to plead, but manage not to. I am half full of him and my body is begging for him to move.

Then he does. No more words. His fingers grip my hips roughly and he slides all the way in, grinding his hips back and forth, levering in and out of me roughly. I push my head to the bed and thrust back to take him. I want to touch myself but don't have permission. I whimper and I sigh and I simply take what he is offering.

"Good girl," he grunts again. As if he's read my mind, he slips a hand under me and gets his fingers slippery with my juices and rubs my tortured clit.

"Sir—"

"You may," he informs me, knowing what I'm going to ask.

I come with a loud sob and then add, though it has nothing to do with our Dom/sub display, just our relationship as a couple: "I'm sorry."

He growls at me. My words have affected him. Carl wedges a finger in my back hole even as his other hand continues to stroke and coax my clitoris to another climax.

I feel the first few tears behind my blindfold. Wish I could take back my childish display. Not feel so petty about Callie's stupid collar. Because this, *this*, is what matters to me.

Just a few more teasing thrusts and I come again, knowing that if I did not have permission he would have said. Our encounter has devolved into normal make-up fucking it seems, and it makes me happy. I've paid my dues and now I can come at will, feel free to push myself back to impale myself on his driving cock.

Freedom...with a blindfold and cuffs. The thought makes me smile.

A second finger slides in my back hole and I'm full of him in both places. So full. So tight.

"You give me one more, Edie," he says.

Gladly.

He does that thing with his hips, that thing that always makes me wetter than I already am. His fingers nudge deep in my ass and I'm coming again, eyes squeezed shut tight behind the blindfold.

I get one more *good girl* before he starts to come, pulling out of me fast, to come on my skin. "Mine," he says, his voice more rough than I've heard it in years.

I drop to the bed. Waiting for the blindfold to come off.

"Sit up." He helps me and when I'm sitting up, he removes the link between the leather cuffs and I can move my hands. Again, he drags something cool—something metallic maybe—along my skin. It disappears before I can identify it. Then, slowly, off comes the blindfold.

"You are not a leather girl," he says. His green eyes are serious. Intent.

"No, Sir."

He picks something up off the nightstand. "Which is why I got you a metal collar."

I stare at it as if I've never seen a collar before. This one is special, though. A glittering white gold with a single O-ring. A lone diamond sparkles to the left of the ring. "I had this made for you. To give you for our six years together. To show everyone..." He smiles at me. "Those who may know what they're looking at and even those who don't—what you mean to me."

I swallow hard. Almost crying but holding on.

He presses the edge of the O-ring so the hinge slides open, allowing him to slip the end of the collar out so he can open it wide to put it around my neck. Then he slides the end back in the ring and the collar is on me—cool beautiful metal—a complete circle.

"Mine," he says again, cocking an eyebrow.

"Yours," I say.

His lips brush mine and I take that kiss so eagerly it's nearly embarrassing. "I know I don't say it enough—at least I don't think I do—but I love you, Edie. In the collar, out of the collar, under my hand or just by my side."

I swallow again. "I love you too."

Somehow the words seem so incompetent in the face of this conversation.

He grins at me. "I was going to give it to you tonight when we got home. But you saw hers and you got all...you know."

I nod, blushing terribly.

"You took all the fun out of it, Edie," he sighs. But I can tell he's not serious.

"I'm sorry—"

He slides a finger up my flank where a hot red stripe still throbs. "That's okay. I found a way to get it back, didn't I?"

I laugh. "Yes, you did." He kisses me again. "Sir," I add, just because I like to hear the word come out of my mouth. It makes me happy.

THROUGH
THE DOOR

Andrea Dale

They say that starting a story with someone walking through a door is a cliché.

But doors and thresholds have powerful symbolism. They represent change, transformation. The simple act of stepping through a doorway can mean leaving your old life or your old self behind.

So I believe my story starts when I walked into the dungeon in a large, anonymous city far, far from where I lived.

I'd done as much research as I could, so I mostly knew what to expect. Downstairs, a dance floor with a throbbing beat, and private rooms for "conversation." Upstairs, the open dungeon, an amusing irony.

The music was faint here, more a beat vibrating the floor like a frat party beneath a movie theater. The primary sounds were thuds and cracks, gasps and shrieks, moans and screams, sobs and the occasional nervous or delighted laugh.

All the sounds went straight to my pussy. My stomach

clenched—in a good way, oh yes—and my nipples beaded to delicious attention, making my silk shirt feel like a wicked, teasing prison.

I watched a woman, tied to a St. Andrew's cross, getting whipped. Her eyes were wide and unfocused, her mouth open. Another cliché—the silent scream—and yet she made no sound. Her response was clear, though: her hips rolled after every strike, her sweet, round ass thrusting back in desperate, eager supplication.

Please, Sir, may I have another? She didn't have to say it aloud.

Not to mention, the person whipping her was another woman.

Unbidden, I felt my back straighten, my breath catch and release, my mouth open just a little, enough for my tongue to dart out and lick my lower lip. *Want.*

My hips rolled, mimicking hers.

So it wasn't much of a surprise to have another woman approach me, ask me if I liked what I saw, and for me to admit was I was here for.

Because the story doesn't need the details, the discussion, the agreements. Just that my safeword was *daffodil* (I have Welsh in me), and that she was amenable.

Eager, even. As was I.

What did I want? she asked me. Oh, what *didn't* I want? Whips and chains, leather and ropes, paddles and whips and flails, oh my!

It was hard to say the word aloud, but finally I managed. "Bondage," I said, that was the main thing. To be tied down—or strapped or chained or whatever—was the crucial act. To be made to believe I was helpless. (I wouldn't be, with the safe-word, but still.) Helpless to whatever she wanted to do to me, pain or pleasure. Helpless to whatever she wanted *me* to do: come or not come, react or wait in excruciating anticipation.

And I wanted it done to me by a woman.

Her face lit up. She was pretty—not classically beautiful, not model thin nor perfectly featured, but she had bright blue eyes and reddish-brown hair, and nipples that thrust even through a red-leather bra. Those eyes had a sinful glint, and her mouth curled in a smile that hinted of sweet cruelty, and that was all it took.

I wanted her to dominate me, to restrain me, to make me feel.

We went to a private room downstairs—I didn't care, but she, solicitous, thought it might be best for my first time. I didn't know how she knew it was my first time, or my first time for what (a club, bondage, pain, a dominant woman). I probably had a look.

As it was, on the way there, I told her my safeword, told her what I wanted. Desired. *Needed.*

The door closed, shutting out all external sound, which surprised me a little.

She didn't ask my name, nor did I ask hers.

"I'll just call you my pet," she said. "My pretty precious pet. Pets always want to please their mistress, don't they? To be praised and stroked when they're good; to be punished when they're bad. When they're naughty."

Her voice was like a rough purr, pitched just for my ears, and my thighs went weak and my pussy swelled and dripped at her words.

I knelt on the padded floor, ass resting on my heels, and said, "I'm sure I've been naughty, yes."

"Oh good," she said with that evil grin. "You have such a scrumptious ass, pet, that just cries out to be blistered. And those breasts...clothespins, I think."

I shuddered.

"But only after you've been tied down," she went on. "Can't have my pretty pet escaping."

The door was right there. I could stand, walk out, walk away, the end.

I turned my head away from it and waited, burning beyond desire.

The room held almost no furniture, certainly no elaborate systems of restraint. No, those were reserved for the public room: horses and racks and cages. There was a padded table here, like one you'd rest on for a massage, but instead she lowered a hook from the ceiling, then rummaged in a cabinet on the wall and selected a set of padded leather restraints for my wrists.

There was more in the cabinet, but I didn't look at that door. I wanted to be surprised. My mind could probably imagine more insidious torture devices than those that lived inside, more deliciously brutal scenarios than those that were possible tonight.

She ratcheted up the hook until my arms were straight overhead but my feet firmly on the floor. She made sure I was safe. I could still close my eyes and pretend I was suspended, dangling helplessly and twisting in the wind.

But I kept my eyes open, because she told me to.

I took a deep breath in through my nose, settling into my precarious, powerless position. I could smell my own sweat—I didn't shave my pits so I was familiar with the odor, but this was tinged with fear...fear and excitement in equal measure. I realized only then that the room had no smell; it must be scrubbed down after every encounter.

Strange, what the brain latches on to in times of intense emotion.

I discovered why I wasn't fully stretched when she nudged my feet apart with the toe of her red stiletto and she knelt to buckle my ankles into a spreader bar. Now my body was taut. Still no threat of permanent damage, but now the feeling of helplessness really kicked in. I couldn't really move or shift much.

Then again, I didn't want to.

Bondage comes in a myriad of forms, and while I've always dreamed of being bound and used by another woman, I knew— knew especially well, now—that psychological bondage is just as powerful.

She said, "Don't move," and I didn't, not when the paddle came down on my ass, not when the flail did, and mostly not when the crop did. And even then, it was more when the crop hit my upper thigh.

And even then, only a flinch and a long, low moan, in a voice I didn't even recognize as my own.

I could only imagine how I looked: arms suspended overhead, my fingers loose and limp; my head bowed, hair obscuring my face as I sucked in deep breaths. Naked, bound, spread, my ass and thighs red and welted.

My nipples tight and pebbled, almost painfully so (I knew better than to think they couldn't feel more pain). The insides of my thighs wet with my juices, all the more frustrating—and a touch humiliating—because I couldn't close my legs.

Except for my harsh breaths, there was silence. Silence, I realized, because she'd told me not to move—another form of bondage, that order—and I had. She was waiting for me to acknowledge my transgression...and realize I would be punished.

I moaned again and began to apologize, but she cut me off, curtly reminding me that unless it came to a safeword, pets didn't speak.

"But I'm glad you know you're going to be punished further," she said. She tapped the crop against my inner thighs, high up where the flesh is most sensitive, and I caught myself before I flinched again. Tap-tap-tapping, higher and higher, until the leather tongue rested against my cunt.

My pussy lips fluttered and my insides clenched. How hard would she hit me? And would I come when she did?

Truth be told, I didn't know if I could come with my legs forced apart like that.

I also didn't know if I was allowed to come. I'd forgotten to bring it up before we started.

I bit my lip, and decided to ask only when it became necessary.

And I held my breath, waiting. There was nothing else I could do.

Her low, breathy laugh startled me, and I tensed, just before she touched the crop to my most vulnerable area. Another tap—not exactly light, but not nearly hard enough to sting or burn. Just the right pressure to arouse me even further.

She wove her fingers into my hair and pulled my head back so she could put her lips near my ear. "That was a warning," she said. "Next time I won't be so kind."

Then she proceeded to do what she'd threatened to at the beginning: she got out the clothespins and decorated my breasts with them. Each innocuous, nasty clip shocked and burned as she made a flower-like halo on the outside of each breast, then four in an inner ring, equidistant.

And then she opened a clothespin in each hand and reached for my hard nipples.

I hadn't told her how sensitive they were.

My whole body stiffened, which was ironic, because that made me thrust my chest out, as if eager, as the clamps bit down. The pain was excruciating, but at the same time, freeing.

Later, I would understand what they meant by *subspace,* that sensation of flying.

As the pain dulled slightly into an aching throb, I feared she'd use the pins elsewhere. But she didn't.

Instead, she circled me, examining me. My breath was harsh, but I looked ahead to watch her as she came in front of me, her eyes first on my ornamented breasts, then on my face.

"Well, look at you," she said. "What a sight. Do you like this feeling, pet? Of not being able to move? Of not being able to do anything about your predicament? Of having to wait, to experience, to turn over all control to me, even when I do this?" And she raised the crop and knocked one of the clothespins off, then two more in rapid succession.

I could barely move, and yet I writhed within my bonds. I couldn't help myself. I didn't cry out, but I clamped my teeth together and keened each time she smacked another one off me, because it hurt even more than when she'd put them on.

It wasn't that, however, that was pushing me so close to the edge. It was her words. She kept up that litany as she struck the pins off, reminding me (as if I could forget!) that I had no power to stop her, to cover myself, to hide, to run.

She talked about what else she'd like to do to me: strap me down on the bench so I couldn't move my hips at all; chain me against a St. Andrew's cross; mummify me in plastic wrap, pinning my limbs together; suspend me in intricate Japanese rope bondage.

Her hypnotic words, her deliciously threatening words, and the pain of the clips being ripped off my breasts inflamed me. My focus narrowed to just that, and the aching heaviness in my cunt, ratcheting tighter.

So when she got to the last two clothespins, the ones on my burning nipples, I imagined what that agony would be like, and she said, "There's nothing you can do. You're helpless."

I started to come before the clothespins came off, my pussy convulsing around emptiness, my clit vibrating. I'd never been able to climax like that before, without direct stimulation, so it took me by surprise, and that made it all the more intense. The pain when the blood rushed back only extended my orgasm, and I bucked and screamed and I—distantly heard—thanked her.

She guided me to a sofa I hadn't even noticed, helped me drink from a bottle of water. When I could hold it by myself, she sipped from her own, cuddling me, my head against her leather-clad breast. I hadn't clued in that she was still clothed until now.

I asked her if I could do anything for her, and she laughed softly and said I'd done quite enough, thank you.

"I'd like to see you again," she said.

"I'm sorry, no," I said. "I'm only in town until tomorrow, on a business trip. I don't think I'll be through here again."

What I didn't say is that I was getting married in two weeks, to the man of my dreams, a man who loved me beyond compare. This wasn't his scene, wasn't his interest, and all I'd wanted was one night he didn't know about to experience my fantasies.

The marks would be gone by the time we said our vows.

They say that when a door closes, another opens.

I thanked her, walked out the door, and gently shut it behind me.

SITTING PRETTY

Alison Tyler

Let's discuss the placement. Positions are extremely important. I'm not talking in bed—doggy-style, missionary or otherwise—but positions in the bar.

The "Number One" girls always choose the preferred stool. Doesn't look like much, I know. Scuffed black leather. Faded silver duct tape covering one deep scratch. Scars and dings on the wooden rungs from the many high heels that have been hooked there. But this is the spot they favor. When you walk in, the stool is the first on your left, at the corner of the bar. Snag this seat and you have the perfect view of the whole place. You can see anyone walking in without craning your neck simply by gazing in the mirror.

The girls sit there. And by "girls," I mean the girls who are tapping the bartenders. Either one. Luke or Dave. The girls sit there and they purr. *I'm the pussy that ate the canary*, they say with their glittery eyes, and they arch and preen and lick their paws. They look around and you can hear them thinking, "This could be *my* bar. This could be *my* man."

Suffice it to say: I don't care much for that stool.

I sit at the other end of the bar. I sit on the far side, my back to the kitchen, almost lost in the shadows. I remember the ghosts of girlfriends past who have sat there, whose hot little bottoms have warmed that stool. I can tick them off if you'd like, but I'd have to use toes as well as fingers and I still might run out of digits. The bar boys get around. Oh, yes they do. They'll own the bar one day, and somehow they manage to stay civil in tight quarters under constant bombardment. They turn, they swivel, they pour, serve, and sneer.

"Amaretto sour."

"Are you fucking kidding me? Do we *look* like a place that would serve an Amaretto sour?"

The latest is Lexi. She's got blonde feathered hair—let's say that together, shall we? *Feathered fucking hair.* She wears bubble-gum pink lip-gloss and her eye shadow is always a shimmery Porn Star Blue. She's doing Dave, and she thinks she's his. She thinks because he slides her a free round every so often, she is in the inner sanctum. This gives her the confidence to flirt with the men on either side of her stool. Lexi believes this makes her more attractive to Dave.

Look, baby, Men think I'm hot.

No, hon. Those men think you're easy.

She doesn't understand the bar boys. She doesn't know that their relationships tend to have short expiration dates. In fact, "relationship" is a bit of a stretch, the word too long for the length of their attention spans.

Lexi stretches. She arches. She purrs.

I sit in the corner, and I sip my whiskey, and I watch.

When Dave passes me, off to get a new bottle of merlot, he tilts his head and gives me a wink. I'm not the cat who ate the canary, but I've swallowed Dave's sword before to the hilt—all eight inches, long and hard. I look at Lexi. She's perched, she's rubbing, ever so gently, her cunt on the bar stool. It wasn't so long ago that she learned her power. *I've got something here that the boys want,* she thought. She doesn't seem to realize that having a slit instead of a piston only means she uses the restroom with the flower. There's no sparkling tiara waiting for her here. There will be no ticker-tape parade.

Lexi turns her attention to the mechanic on her right. He's got massive hands, gnarled knuckles, a white shadow where his ring used to be. Lexi toys with the chain around her neck, tugs the chrome heart. I've seen her slip the cold metal pendant into her mouth and suck, a nervous habit. A coy girl trick.

Jonathan knows she doesn't want him. He's a placeholder, a paper doll cutout that she can play with while she waits for Dave to get off. To get off and then get off in her. *Maybe behind the bar tonight, baby. Maybe in the back of your truck.* Yet she trots out that old used trope of flirting with a man to make her lover see her worth.

Doll, I want to say. *You didn't invent this little dramedy. And other girls have played your role with so much more feeling. So much more depth.*

Dave returns with the merlot and he leans into me slightly, his hips bumping mine as he moves behind the bar. Our eyes meet. I think of the way his cock feels in my mouth, the rounded tip, the thick shaft.

I wonder what Lexi would say if she knew I've tasted her juices on Dave's cock. It's almost like I've fucked her. She's got a bite to her sweetness, a sharp flavor that suits her. She pretends she's a pussycat, but she's all barracuda beneath the skin.

The bar is bustling. Dave is hustling. Lexi perches and flirts and twitters. I enjoy the view, thinking of all those girls before her. Thinking of all those girls who will snag that seat in the future. I'm not jealous. I'm not the type. But when Dave refills my glass, he says, "You know what that girl needs?"

"An ass-whooping," I say, and he grins and nods. He's got a shadow going. I love the way those whisper-whiskers feel when they graze my skin.

"You up for it?" he asks me, and my cock gets hard.

It's two a.m. at my place when he brings her over. She's shiny around the edges now, sleepy but ready. She says, "Hiya, Hank," as if her charms will work on me. How'd Dave get her here? *Wanna stop by for a drink at my friend's house? You know Hank, right?* Dave doesn't like to drink at the bar, even after closing. It doesn't set a good precedent when the owner decimates the stock.

I've got the bottle of top-shelf whiskey on the coffee table and three antique crystal glasses set out. A silver bucket of ice if that's her style. She's a cosmo girl, I know. A pink drinker. But I don't have the accoutrements. It's whiskey—neat or on the rocks, if you must—or nothing.

Dave says, "Lexi doesn't know what you do."

"Yeah, Hank." She's so perky. "Dave made me guess on the way over. I couldn't figure it out." I can hear her voice in my head. *Is he an architect? An engineer? A reference librarian?*

"I'm a refinisher," I say. She looks around my place. Sees the furniture, appraises the workmanship. "I strip things down to the bare, to the core, and then I rebuild."

The way I say the words makes her straighten up. She can hear a threat in my tone—or if not a threat, a promise. She's sitting on my chair the way she sits at the bar, her pussy right on the lip of it, balancing on her power. She rubs back and forth. I don't even think she knows she's moving.

"You do all the furniture in the room?" she asks, looking around, nervous suddenly.

I nod.

She licks her lips, sips her drink, chatters the ice cubes in the glass. Dave is relaxed, leg crossed so his ankle rests on his knee, watching me. I know what he wants to see. There's no reason to put off the inevitable.

"Dave says you've been a bad girl," I tell Lexi, and her nervous twitching movements suddenly stop.

"What did you say?"

I enunciate carefully. "Dave tells me you've been a bad, bad girl." I add the second *bad* for emphasis.

She looks shocked at Dave, who doesn't move, doesn't flinch. He takes a drink and smiles, nothing nervous in his attitude. Dave likes to be here. He's sitting in his black leather chair. I finished that one just for him.

"Did you, Dave?" she can't decide how to play this scene. Does she act all giggly about it? Or become incensed, her reputation soiled. I've stripped her first layer, without any effort at all.

Dave nods, but gives her no additional assistance. This is where we find out what Lexi has in her. Will she storm out? Throw her drink at Dave? Call me an old lecherous bastard? There are a slew of possibilities, but I'm fairly secure in the end result of the evening. Or morning.

She worries her bottom lip. She squints her blue eyes at me.

"Why would you say that?" she asks, and the question is posed to both of us.

I decide to be the one to answer. "You act like you want to be Dave's girl," I tell her, "and then you squirm on that bar stool and send off your scent. Do you think he doesn't see you flirting like that?"

"I was... I mean, I wasn't..."

"You were." There's no need to argue. She seems to understand this.

"I wouldn't have done anything with them." She says this with a pout.

"Does that make it better?"

Not many of us get to confront our true selves. We dress up. We go to the bar. We mingle with the rest of the humans. And we wear our masks. I've taken Lexi's away. She is a tangle of nerves, a visible twitching ball of raw emotions.

Her ice cubes are clinking together again. She's at a juncture. Will she stay or will she go?

"No," she says, and she looks at the coffee table, which I found one day on a dump run and refurbished over a period of months. The sheen is pure love and sweat equity. She runs her fingertip over the rim. "No," she says again, and we're right there—at the pivotal place. Didn't take us that long at all. She says, "That doesn't make it better."

I stand and walk to her side. I take her drink and set the glass on the tray. I help her to her feet and bring her back to my chair, where I sit once more and stand her between my legs.

"Dave says you've been a bad girl," I repeat. The cadence now is like a song. Lexi starts to tear up; years of practice make crying on command one of the tricks in her magic bag. I shake my head. "Sweet girl," I tell her simply, "you haven't earned your tears yet."

She's staring at me with her wide blue eyes. Her plump bottom lip is ripe and bitable. Her fluttery halter is made of silk ruffles. She says, "What do you want me to do, Hank? What am I supposed to do about it?" She knows better than to be aggressive, but there's still an edge to her tone, like there's a bite to her taste.

That's all I need. I look over at Dave, who hasn't moved, but he's excited. I can tell. His fine cheekbones have a warmth to them, a heat. I take Lexi and bend her across my lap. This is it. This is the start or the end. She is malleable and willing. She has given in, given up, joined the program.

Lexi's over my lap and I lift her little floral mini skirt and stare down at her ass. She's got on a thong. Of course, she does. A lemon-yellow thong trimmed in white lace. I let a hand rest on her ass, and I look at Dave again. He's grinning. This is the best part for him. He loves to watch me punish his girls. He'll do almost anything to get to this point. And I'll do anything for Dave.

I don't spank her right away, though. I rest my large hand on her ass, and I say, "What's going to happen, Lexi?"

She has her palms on the floor, bracing herself. Her hair falls over her face. She knows, and Dave knows, and I know. But we have to hear Lexi say the words. It's part of the routine. She's got to give in.

"What do you think I'm going to do?"

She doesn't want to talk. She's convinced herself that this is acceptable—her being over my lap and all. She's had the inner dialogue, has made all sorts of devil's deals with herself. If this is what Dave really wants. Maybe he's more kinky than she thought. And blah blah blah. But she didn't think I'd make her spell out the situation. I crave clarity.

"What do you think I'm going to do?" I ask her. My voice is like the finest grade of sandpaper, hardly rough at all.

"You're going to…you're going to…" She turns her head to face Dave, but I can't have that.

"He doesn't have the answer," I tell her. "Neither does the floor. Or your little heart-shaped pendant. What am I going to do?"

"You're going to spank me." The words are a rush, a tumble, ice cubes melting in a crystal glass.

"And what are you going to do?"

"What am I...?" It's so hard for her. I want to tell her that she's not alone. It's hard for all of Dave's girls.

"What are you going to do?" I repeat. "As my hand comes down on your firm little ass, what are *you* going to do?"

"I'm going to cry."

There. We're all on the same page. I tug at the floss of her thong. She feels the pull against her asshole. A divine shiver works through her. I know that if I were to slip my fingers between her legs, I'd find a puddle. I could make her guess the rest of the evening's events, but I decide to wait. We'll begin the begin.

I slap her ass once. Hard. She sucks in her breath. I can almost hear her thoughts. *That wasn't so bad. I can take this. I can handle this.* I slap her again, quickly, and the thoughts begin to come faster. *How long will he spank me? How much will this hurt?* And again. She exhales. She was holding her breath without realizing. I give in to myself and start smacking her ass rhythmically. This isn't only about her after all. Dave is leaning forward on his chair to watch. I'm turning the key that opens Dave up. The watching. I put on a proper show. When Lexi starts to squirm, searching for purchase with her cunt against my knee, I grab both her wrists and pin them at the small of her back. I have clocked her arching at the bar. Now I bend her like a bow, and I motion to Dave.

He comes forward, stands in front of her. She lifts her head and he brushes the hair away from her pretty face.

"Do you think you could suck him while I spank you?" I ask Lexi. I ask it the way I might ask for a second round at the bar, in an if-it's-not-too-much-trouble sort of way.

Lexi opens her mouth. Dave undoes his jeans. In seconds, she's sucking him, slurping him, wetting his cock all over, and I'm punishing her ass for her in a fast, powerful manner. I love the way her bottom looks now. All red and blushing. As she works Dave's cock, I tug the thread of lace between her asscheeks, stimulating her asshole again. I tug over and over. She groans around Dave's rod, and I decide it's time to press forward. I slip the thong down her thighs and dip two fingers into her split. She's drenched, as I expected.

"Do you know what I like to do to a bad girl after I spank her?" I ask Lexi.

She mumbles a word that sounds like "No," around Dave's cock. Dave moans.

"I fuck her asshole." I touch Lexi's as I say the words.

Lexi pulls off Dave's cock and looks at me. Then she looks up at Dave. She's panting, and we can all smell the perfume of her arousal.

"Let's go to the bedroom," I say.

On my big mattress, Lexi's in the center. Dave has to fuck her first. He *has* to. Watching her get a spanking almost finished him off. Her blow job was icing. Thinking about me taking her asshole is too much for him to consider. Dave gets her doggy-style and he plunges his cock into her pussy. I stand across the room and keep tabs on the action. Lexi locks her eyes on me. She heard what I said before, and I know she's thinking about what I told her. Has she had her asshole fucked before? I'm guessing no. I'm guessing that Lexi will blow you like a pro, that she will spread her legs over her head if you want, but that up until tonight, her tight pucker has been off limits.

Dave fucks her, and leans forward, biting her shoulders, grinding his hips against hers. He is so excited, he can't help but come quickly, pounding into her as he reaches his limits. Then he sighs and pulls out. His eyes meet mine. *What's next?* He's asking without words. *What do you want, Hank? What do you want from me?*

I nod to the living room and he grabs up a blanket from the bed and heads out there. He doesn't mind. Dave and I have that special sort of relationship with no jealousy and no pain. We serve each other's needs. Right now, he's willing to give me what I want: Alone time with Lexi.

Her eyes are still huge at the thought of me taking her tight little asshole. I come to the bed and I say, "I'm going to tie you down for this. Are you okay with that?"

She nods, so serious, then asks, "Will it hurt?"

"No, baby. Not the ass-fucking. But I want to whip you a little more first."

She sucks in her breath and nods again. I've opened up a whole new world for Lexi. She puts her hands out, waiting. I have the cuffs ready. I bind her like the pro I am.

As I stretch out her body, preparing her for my belt, I start to realize my feelings have changed. I have taken care of Dave's girls so often that the movements had lost a bit of their thrill. But Lexi's different. I suddenly find myself wanting to make this last. I show her my belt. I bring the metal buckle to her lips. She shakes her hair out of her face and she kisses the silver. My cock fucking throbs.

I double the leather and snap the belt in the air. Then I stripe her. Lexi's skin is still glowing from the over-the-knee spanking I gave her. The stripes manage to stand out in bold relief even over the pinkness on her plump cheeks. After I land ten, I drop the belt and rub her ass with my palms. Lexi draws her knees up under her body, and I see what she's doing. The concept of me fucking her hole is mesmerizing to her. Unconsciously or consciously—I don't know which—she's splitting herself for me. I grab the lube and get ready.

"I've never…" she starts, confirming what I thought before.

"I know."

I drizzle the lube between her asscheeks and then I slowly begin to toy with her hole. Lexi moans and arches her body as if I am playing with her clit, arching differently from how she moves in the bar. Oh, dear lord. She's one of those girls. I bet I could make her come if I kept doing this. But my cock is demanding satisfaction. I won't be able to hold off forever.

When I'm sure she's nice and lubed—when my fingers slide easily inside her tight hole—I strip and join her on the bed. Lexi's wrists are still cuffed, but she continues to make my life easier. She lifts her ass for me, parts her legs. I spread her wide and press the head of my cock at her opening.

"You ready?" I ask, even though we both know she's more than ready. She's dying for this.

"Oh, god, yes. Hank, fuck me. Fuck my ass."

I push hard, and she cries out. I think of Dave in the other room. He's got to be listening and imagining what we're doing in here. He's probably jacking himself off on the sofa. I know I would be.

Lexi starts to fuck me back, and my estimation of her rises again. She's an active participant, unlike some of Dave's girls who have just taken it. Accepted their fate. This is exciting to me. I hold still, and Lexi fucks my cock with her ass. My breathing speeds up. I feel like the virgin for once. How'd a girl like her, a girl I thought I could see through, change the power? I don't even care at this point. I let Lexi fuck me hard and fast, and right when I know I'm at my limits, I reach my hand under her to tweak her clit. I press my thumb directly on her trigger, and she climaxes like a dream. Her whole body seems to contract and release, and my cock receives the pleasure in waves.

I come on the end of her orgasm, filling her ass with my spend. She dissolves onto my sheets, turning her head, seeming to bury herself in my pillows. I pull out, undo her wrists, kiss her parted lips.

Then I take her to the shower, to wash her. I know Dave is probably asleep on my couch, his fist wet with his own come. He won't bother us, won't think to disturb us.

Lexi's ass is still lovely and red. I shampoo her hair; I scrub off the rest of her makeup. When I towel her dry, she is luminous. I dress again, then stand her in front of the mirror in my bathroom and I reach for my scissors. Lexi stares at me, but she doesn't say a word. In a few minutes, I've changed her hairstyle, gotten rid of those long feathers, given her a neat, slightly punkish cut. I always know. That's a gift more than a skill. I can see a piece of furniture and understand what I have to do. I can see a girl and the same feeling runs through me.

Lexi's too-short skirt, her skimpy halter, seem inappropriate now. I get her one of my white work shirts and she buttons it up, rolls the sleeves, stares at me expectantly, then over my shoulder.

She's looking at the strop on the back of my door.

"Not for now," I say, shaking my head. "You're not ready."

Everything about her is different. She's the human embodiment of my best work. I saw the raw material. I made something new without destroying the old.

"Can I sit next to you tomorrow?" she asks me. Her voice is hushed, subdued. I tousle her hair. I kiss her lips. "I'd expect nothing else," I say.

"Can I ask you another question Hank?"

I wait for it.

"Why don't you ever fix that bar stool? The scarred one."

I lead her by the hand to my studio. We'll let Dave sleep in peace. "I only take the time to fix the things I care about," I say. "I don't waste my time."

She has her hand on my belt. She's pulling loose the buckle. "Fix me again," she asks.

I push her hand away. My cock is hard. I don't know how we're going to make this work. Lexi, and Dave and myself. But I've got all the tools, and I've got the time. And in my world, that's all anyone needs.

ABOUT THE AUTHORS

VIDA BAILEY lives in Ireland and occasionally takes breaks from her busy schedule of procrastinating to write a saucy story or two. You can find her upcoming work in Kristina Wright's *Sweet and Sexy* anthology and Alison Tyler's *Big Book of Bondage, Sudden Sex* and *Morning Noon and Night*.

KRISTY LIN BILLUNI (sexygrammar.com) is a writing teacher and ten-year owner of a small business called Sexy Grammar, which arouses writers with free online lessons, editing and collaboration services. Before she found her life's work as The Sexy Grammarian, she tramped through San Francisco's and Boston's kink and sex-work undergrounds.

LAILA BLAKE (www.lailablake.com) is a bi-lingual German native with an MA in applied linguistics, working as a translator and English teacher in Cologne, Germany. She spends her evenings and weekends penning character-driven romance and erotica and is just about to sell the rights to her first novel.

RACHEL KRAMER BUSSEL (rachelkramerbussel.com) is the editor of *Please, Sir; Yes, Sir; He's on Top; Cheeky Spanking Stories; Spanked, Bottoms Up; Anything for You: Erotica for Kinky Couples; Twice the Pleasure: Bisexual Women's Erotica; Baby Got Back: Anal Erotica; Best Bondage Erotica 2011, 2012, 2013* and many other erotica anthologies.

HEIDI CHAMPA (heidichampa.blogspot.com) has been published in numerous anthologies including *Best Women's Erotica 2010, Playing With Fire, Irresistible* and *Best Erotic Romance 2013*. She has also steamed up the pages of Bust Magazine. She can also be found at Clean Sheets, Ravenous Romance, Oysters and Chocolate and The Erotic Woman.

ANDREA DALE (andreadaleauthor.com) has been called a "legendary erotica heavy-hitter" by the über-legendary Violet Blue. Her work has appeared in twenty year's-best volumes as well as about one hundred other anthologies from Soul's Road Press, Harlequin Spice and Cleis Press. She's fascinated by doorways and portals, and the mysteries and opportunities they represent.

KIKIDELOVELY (kikidelovely.wordpress.com) is a queer femme writer/performer whose work has appeared in various publications, including *Best Lesbian Erotica 2011* and *2012, The Big Book of Bondage*, and *Say Please: Lesbian BDSM Erotica*. Kiki's passions include magical realism, the Oxford comma and taking on research for her writing.

AMY DILLON's fiction has appeared in the anthologies *Her Way: Romantic Femdom Stories* and *Asking for It: Female Submissive Erotica*. She lives in California with her boyfriend, a cat and at least one yummy pair of boots.

BENJAMIN ELIOT loves his wife, his kids, and his old piece-of-crap car. For the record, he can fix a toilet and even install a faucet. Benjamin was never one for fairy tales, but in college he found he could really get into a good meaty Greek myth. His work has appeared in *Alison's Wonderland*.

BEATRIX ELLROY is an ex-librarian book-hound with a love of words: the dirtier the better. This is her entry into the world of erotica as a writer. Previous work has included everything from articles about computer games to literary fiction, but erotica is her passion and her weakness.

As a naughty girl on a journey of self-discovery as an erotic writer, TAMSIN FLOWERS (tamsinflowers.com) is as keen to entertain her readers as she is to explore every aspect of male and female erotica.

GRAYDANCER's (graydancer.com) sex-positive fiction and nonfiction has appeared in many anthologies. He is a sex educator, performer and activist and part of the Erotication websites. He is known for his "Ropecast" (a kinky podcast) and kinky unconferences ("GRUEs") throughout the world.

TILLY HUNTER (tillyhunter.co.uk) is a British author and newspaper journalist with a wicked imagination and a fondness for stories of good food, simple living and BDSM. Her work has been published by Xcite Books and the websites Every Night Erotica and Oysters & Chocolate.

D. L. KING's (dlkingerotica.blogspot.com) short stories have appeared in titles such as *Best Women's Erotica; One Night*

Only; Luscious; Please, Ma'am and many others. She is also the editor of *Seductress, The Harder She Comes, Spankalicious, Voyeur Eyes Only, Carnal Machines, Spank!, The Sweetest Kiss* and *Where the Girls Are.*

ANNABETH LEONG (annabethleong.blogspot.com) has written erotica of many flavors—dark, romantic, kinky, vanilla, straight, lesbian, bi and ménage. She frequently gets schooled at bondage cons for not using hemp rope. Her work has been published by Cleis, Xcite, Circlet, Coming Together and others.

K. LYNN (writerklynn.com) has been a longtime fan of the erotica market, sneaking in reading time when no one was watching. She enjoys subverting the gender stereotypes in her writing and looks forward to exploring that more in the future. When she's not writing short stories, she's working on her novels.

SOMMER MARSDEN's (sommermarsden.blogspot.com) been called "...one of the top storytellers in the erotica genre" (Violet Blue) and "Unapologetic" (Alison Tyler). Her erotic novels include *Boys Next Door, Learning to Drown* and *Restless Spirit.*

GISELLE RENARDE (donutsdesires.blogspot.com) is author of the 2012 Rainbow Award–winning trans-lesbian romance *The Red Satin Collection,* 2011 Rainbow Awards Honorable Mention *My Mistress' Thighs: Erotic Transgender Fiction and Poetry,* as well as *Anonymous, Ondine, Audrey & Lawrence* and many dozens of e-books.

TERESA NOELLE ROBERTS (teresanoelleroberts.com) writes sexy stories for lusty romantics of all persuasions. Look for her BDSM romance *Knowing the Ropes* from Samhain. Her work has appeared in *The Big Book of Bondage*; *Best Bondage Erotica 2011, 2012* and *2013*; and other provocatively titled anthologies.

KATHLEEN TUDOR is a writer and editor who sometimes walks on the wild side. Her work has appeared in anthologies from Cleis, Xcite, Mischief HarperCollins and many more. Watch out for news of new releases as well as hot stories on her website, KathleenTudor.com.

SOPHIA VALENTI (sophiavalenti.blogspot.com) is the author of *Indecent Desires*, an erotic novella of spanking and submission. Her fiction has appeared in a number of kinky erotica anthologies, including *The Big Book of Bondage*, *Twisted* and *Cuffed*.

SASKIA WALKER (saskiawalker.co.uk) is a British author whose short fiction appears in over eighty anthologies. Her erotic novels include *Rampant, The Harlot, The Libertine* and *The Jezebel*. Saskia lives in Yorkshire, England with her real-life hero, Mark, and a house full of stray felines.

ABOUT
THE EDITOR

Called "a trollop with a laptop" by *East Bay Express,* "a literary siren" by Good Vibrations and "the mistress of literary erotica" by Violet Blue, **ALISON TYLER** is naughty and she knows it.

Over the past two decades, Ms. Tyler has written more than twenty-five explicit novels, including *Tiffany Twisted, Melt with You,* and *The ESP Affair.* Her novels and short stories have been translated into Japanese, Dutch, German, Italian, Norwegian, Spanish and Greek. When not writing sultry short stories, she edits erotic anthologies, including *Alison's Wonderland, Kiss My Ass, Skirting the Issue* and *Torn.*

Ms. Tyler is loyal to coffee (black), lipstick (red) and tequila (straight). She has tattoos, but no piercings; a wicked tongue, but a quick smile; and bittersweet memories, but no regrets. She believes it won't rain if she doesn't bring an umbrella, prefers hot and dry to cold and wet, and loves to spout her favorite motto: You can sleep when you're dead. She chooses Led Zeppelin over the Beatles, the Cure over NIN, and the Stones over everyone.

Yet although she appreciates good rock, she has a pitiful weakness for '80s hair bands.

In all things important, she remains faithful to her partner of eighteen years, but she still can't choose just one perfume.

More from Alison Tyler

Buy 4 books, Get 1 FREE*

Frenzy
60 Stories of Sudden Sex
Edited by Alison Tyler

"Toss out the roses and box of candies. This isn't a prolonged seduction. This is slammed against the wall in an alleyway sex, and it's all that much hotter for it."
—Erotica Readers & Writers Association
ISBN 978-1-57344-331-9 $14.95

Best Bondage Erotica
Edited by Alison Tyler

Always playful and dangerously explicit, these arresting fantasies grab you, tie you down, and never let you go.
ISBN 978-1-57344-173-5 $15.95

Afternoon Delight
Erotica for Couples
Edited by Alison Tyler

"Alison Tyler evokes a world of heady sensuality where fantasies are fearlessly explored and dreams gloriously realized."
—Barbara Pizio, Executive Editor,
Penthouse Variations
ISBN 978-1-57344-341-8 $14.95

Got a Minute?
60 Second Erotica
Edited by Alison Tyler

"Classy but very, very dirty, this is one of the few very truly indispensable filth anthologies around." —*UK Forum*
ISBN 978-1-57344-404-0 $14.95

Playing with Fire
Taboo Erotica
Edited by Alison Tyler

"Alison Tyler has managed to find the best stories from the best authors, and create a book of fantasies that—if you're lucky enough, or determined enough—just might come true." —Clean Sheets
ISBN 978-1-57344-348-7 $14.95

* Free book of equal or lesser value. Shipping and applicable sales tax extra.
Cleis Press • (800) 780-2279 • orders@cleispress.com
www.cleispress.com

Happy Endings Forever and Ever

Buy 4 books,
Get 1 *FREE**

Dark Secret Love
A Story of Submission
By Alison Tyler

Inspired by her own BDSM exploits and private diaries, Alison Tyler draws on twenty-five years of penning sultry stories to create a scorchingly hot work of fiction, a memoir-inspired novel with reality at its core. A modern-day *Story of O*, a *9 1/2 Weeks*-style journey fueled by lust, longing and the search for true love.
ISBN 978-1-57344-956-4 $16.95

High-Octane Heroes
Erotic Romance for Women
Edited by Delilah Devlin

One glance and your heart will melt—these chiseled, brave men will ignite your fantasies with their courage and charisma. Award-winning romance writer Delilah Devlin has gathered stories of hunky, red-blooded guys who enter danger zones in the name of duty, honor, country and even love.
ISBN 978-1-57344-969-4 $15.95

Duty and Desire
Military Erotic Romance
Edited by Kristina Wright

The only thing stronger than the call of duty is the call of desire. *Duty and Desire* enlists a team of hot-blooded men and women from every branch of the military who serve their country and follow their hearts.
ISBN 978-1-57344-823-9 $15.95

Smokin' Hot Firemen
Erotic Romance Stories for Women
Edited by Delilah Devlin

Delilah delivers tales of these courageous men breaking down doors to steal readers' hearts! *Smokin' Hot Firemen* imagines the romantic possibilities of being held against a massively muscled chest by a man whose mission is to save lives and serve *every* need.
ISBN 978-1-57344-934-2 $15.95

Only You
Erotic Romance for Women
Edited by Rachel Kramer Bussel

Only You is full of tenderness, raw passion, love, longing and the many emotions that kindle true romance. The couples in *Only You* test the boundaries of their love to make their relationships stronger.
ISBN 978-1-57344-909-0 $15.95

* Free book of equal or lesser value. Shipping and applicable sales tax extra.
Cleis Press • (800) 780-2279 • orders@cleispress.com
www.cleispress.com

Many More Than Fifty Shades of Erotica

Buy 4 books, Get 1 FREE*

Please, Sir
Erotic Stories of Female Submission
Edited by Rachel Kramer Bussel

If you liked *Fifty Shades of Grey*, you'll love the explosive stories of *Please, Sir*. These damsels delight in the pleasures of taking risks to be rewarded by the men who know their deepest desires. Find out why nothing is as hot as the power of the words "Please, Sir."
ISBN 978-1-57344-389-0 $14.95

Yes, Sir
Erotic Stories of Female Submission
Edited by Rachel Kramer Bussel

Bound, gagged or spanked—or controlled with just a glance—these lucky women experience the breathtaking thrills of sexual submission. *Yes, Sir* shows that pleasure is best when dispensed by a firm hand.
ISBN 978-1-57344-310-4 $15.95

He's on Top
Erotic Stories of Male Dominance and Female Submission
Edited by Rachel Kramer Bussel

As true tops, the bossy hunks in these stories understand that BDSM is about exulting in power that is freely yielded. These kinky stories celebrate women who know exactly what they want.
ISBN 978-1-57344-270-1 $14.95

Best Bondage Erotica 2013
Edited by Rachel Kramer Bussel

Let *Best Bondage Erotica 2013* be your kinky playbook to erotic restraint—from silk ties and rope to shiny cuffs, blindfolds and so much more. These stories of forbidden desire will captivate, shock and arouse you.
ISBN 978-1-57344-897-0 $15.95

Luscious
Stories of Anal Eroticism
Edited by Alison Tyler

Discover all the erotic possibilities that exist between the sheets and between the cheeks in this daring collection. "Alison Tyler is an author to rely on for steamy, sexy page turners! Try her!"—Powell's Books
ISBN 978-1-57344-760-7 $15.95

* Free book of equal or lesser value. Shipping and applicable sales tax extra.
Cleis Press • (800) 780-2279 • orders@cleispress.com
www.cleispress.com

Unleash Your Favorite Fantasies

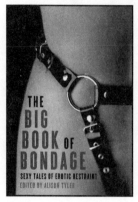

Buy 4 books, Get 1 FREE*

The Big Book of Bondage
Sexy Tales of Erotic Restraint
Edited by Alison Tyler

Nobody likes bondage more than editrix Alison Tyler, who is fascinated with the ecstasies of giving up, giving in, and entrusting one's pleasure (and pain) into the hands of another. Delve into a world of unrestrained passion, where heart-stopping dynamics will thrill and inspire you.
ISBN 978-1-57344-907-6 $15.95

Hurts So Good
Unrestrained Erotica
Edited by Alison Tyler
Intricately secured by ropes, locked in handcuffs or bound simply by a lover's command, the characters of *Hurts So Good* find themselves in the throes of pleasurable restraint in this indispensible collection by prolific, award-winning editor Alison Tyler.
ISBN 978-1-57344-723-2 $14.95

Caught Looking
Erotic Tales of Voyeurs and Exhibitionists
Edited by Alison Tyler
and Rachel Kramer Bussel

These scintillating fantasies take the reader inside a world where people get to show off, watch, and feel the vicarious thrill of sex times two, their erotic power multiplied by the eyes of another.
ISBN 978-1-57344-256-5 $14.95

Hide and Seek
Erotic Tales of Voyeurs and Exhibitionists
Edited by Rachel Kramer Bussel
and Alison Tyler

Whether putting on a deliberate show for an eager audience or peeking into the hidden sex lives of their neighbors, these show-offs and shy types go all out in their quest for the perfect peep show.
ISBN 978-1-57344-419-4 $14.95

One Night Only
Erotic Encounters
Edited by Violet Blue

"Passion and lust play by different rules in *One Night Only*. These are stories about what happens when we have just that one opportunity to ask for what we want—and we take it… Enjoy the adventure."
—Violet Blue
ISBN 978-1-57344-756-0 $14.95

---

* Free book of equal or lesser value. Shipping and applicable sales tax extra.
Cleis Press • (800) 780-2279 • orders@cleispress.com
www.cleispress.com

Red Hot Erotic Romance

Buy 4 books, Get 1 *FREE*

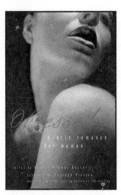

Obsessed
Erotic Romance for Women
Edited by Rachel Kramer Bussel

These stories sizzle with the kind of obsession that is fueled by our deepest desires, the ones that hold couples together, the ones that haunt us and don't let go. Whether just-blooming passions, rekindled sparks or reinvented relationships, these lovers put the object of their obsession first.
ISBN 978-1-57344-718-8 $14.95

Passion
Erotic Romance for Women
Edited by Rachel Kramer Bussel

Love and sex have always been intimately intertwined—and *Passion* shows just how delicious the possibilities are when they mingle in this sensual collection edited by award-winning author Rachel Kramer Bussel.
ISBN 978-1-57344-415-6 $14.95

Girls Who Bite
Lesbian Vampire Erotica
Edited by Delilah Devlin

Bestselling romance writer Delilah Devlin and her contributors add fresh girl-on-girl blood to the pantheon of the paranormal. The stories in *Girls Who Bite* are varied, unexpected, and soul-scorching.
ISBN 978-1-57344-715-7 $14.95

Irresistible
Erotic Romance for Couples
Edited by Rachel Kramer Bussel

This prolific editor has gathered the most popular fantasies and created a sizzling, no-holds-barred collection of explicit encounters in which couples turn their deepest desires into reality.
978-1-57344-762-1 $14.95

Heat Wave
Hot, Hot, Hot Erotica
Edited by Alison Tyler

What could be sexier or more seductive than bare, sun-warmed skin? Bestselling erotica author Alison Tyler gathers explicit stories of summer sex bursting with the sweet eroticism of swimsuits, sprinklers, and ripe strawberries.
ISBN 978-1-57344-710-2 $15.95

★ Free book of equal or lesser value. Shipping and applicable sales tax extra.
Cleis Press • (800) 780-2279 • orders@cleispress.com
www.cleispress.com

Bestselling Erotica for Couples

Buy 4 books,
Get 1 *FREE**

Sweet Life
Erotic Fantasies for Couples
Edited by Violet Blue

Your ticket to a front row seat for first-time spankings, breathtaking role-playing scenes, sex parties, women who strap it on and men who love to take it, not to mention threesomes of every combination.
ISBN 978-1-57344-133-9 $14.95

Sweet Life 2
Erotic Fantasies for Couples
Edited by Violet Blue

"This is a we-did-it-you-can-too anthology of real couples playing out their fantasies." —Lou Paget, author of *365 Days of Sensational Sex*
ISBN 978-1-57344-167-4 $15.95

Sweet Love
Erotic Fantasies for Couples
Edited by Violet Blue

"If you ever get a chance to try out your number-one fantasies in real life—and I assure you, there will be more than one—say yes. It's well worth it. May this book, its adventurous authors, and the daring and satisfied characters be your guiding inspiration."—Violet Blue
ISBN 978-1-57344-381-4 $14.95

Afternoon Delight
Erotica for Couples
Edited by Alison Tyler

"Alison Tyler evokes a world of heady sensuality where fantasies are fearlessly explored and dreams gloriously realized."
—Barbara Pizio, Executive Editor, *Penthouse Variations*
ISBN 978-1-57344-341-8 $14.95

Three-Way
Erotic Stories
Edited by Alison Tyler

"Three means more of everything. Maybe I'm greedy, but when it comes to sex, I like more. More fingers. More tongues. More limbs. More tangling and wrestling on the mattress." —from the introduction
ISBN 978-1-57344-193-3 $15.95

---

* Free book of equal or lesser value. Shipping and applicable sales tax extra.
Cleis Press • (800) 780-2279 • orders@cleispress.com
www.cleispress.com

Best Erotica Series

"Gets racier every year."—*San Francisco Bay Guardian*

Buy 4 books,
Get 1 *FREE**

Best Women's Erotica 2014
Edited by Violet Blue
ISBN 978-1-62778-003-2 $15.95

Best Women's Erotica 2013
Edited by Violet Blue
ISBN 978-1-57344-898-7 $15.95

Best Women's Erotica 2012
Edited by Violet Blue
ISBN 978-1-57344-755-3 $15.95

Best Bondage Erotica 2014
Edited by Rachel Kramer Bussel
ISBN 978-1-62778-012-4 $15.95

Best Bondage Erotica 2013
Edited by Rachel Kramer Bussel
ISBN 978-1-57344-897-0 $15.95

Best Bondage Erotica 2012
Edited by Rachel Kramer Bussel
ISBN 978-1-57344-754-6 $15.95

Best Lesbian Erotica 2014
Edited by Kathleen Warnock
ISBN 978-1-62778-002-5 $15.95

Best Lesbian Erotica 2013
Edited by Kathleen Warnock
Selected and introduced by
Jewelle Gomez
ISBN 978-1-57344-896-3 $15.95

Best Lesbian Erotica 2012
Edited by Kathleen Warnock
Selected and introduced by
Sinclair Sexsmith
ISBN 978-1-57344-752-2 $15.95

Best Gay Erotica 2014
Edited by Larry Duplechan
Selected and introduced by Joe Manetti
ISBN 978-1-62778-001-8 $15.95

Best Gay Erotica 2013
Edited by Richard Labonté
Selected and introduced by Paul Russell
ISBN 978-1-57344-895-6 $15.95

Best Gay Erotica 2012
Edited by Richard Labonté
Selected and introduced by
Larry Duplechan
ISBN 978-1-57344-753-9 $15.95

Best Fetish Erotica
Edited by Cara Bruce
ISBN 978-1-57344-355-5 $15.95

Best Bisexual Women's Erotica
Edited by Cara Bruce
ISBN 978-1-57344-320-3 $15.95

Best Lesbian Bondage Erotica
Edited by Tristan Taormino
ISBN 978-1-57344-287-9 $16.95

* Free book of equal or lesser value. Shipping and applicable sales tax extra.
Cleis Press • (800) 780-2279 • orders@cleispress.com
www.cleispress.com

Ordering is easy! Call us toll free or fax us to place your MC/VISA order.
You can also mail the order form below with payment to:
Cleis Press, 2246 Sixth St., Berkeley, CA 94710.

ORDER FORM

QTY	TITLE	PRICE

SUBTOTAL _____

SHIPPING _____

SALES TAX _____

TOTAL _____

Add $3.95 postage/handling for the first book ordered and $1.00 for each additional book. Outside North America, please contact us for shipping rates. California residents add 9% sales tax. Payment in U.S. dollars only.

* Free book of equal or lesser value. Shipping and applicable sales tax extra.

Cleis Press • Phone: (800) 780-2279 • Fax: (510) 845-8001
orders@cleispress.com • www.cleispress.com
You'll find more great books on our website

Follow us on Twitter @cleispress • Friend/fan us on Facebook